DISCARD

The One Who Came Back

· · · The One Who Came Back

by Joann Mazzio

Houghton Mifflin Company

BOSTON 1992

Library of Congress Cataloging-in-Publication Data

Mazzio, Joann.
  The one who came back / by Joann Mazzio.
    p. cm.
  Summary: When his best friend Eddie Chavez disappears after they
have spent the day together in the mountains of New Mexico, fifteen-
year-old Alex cannot get anyone to believe his story and is even
suspected of murdering the missing boy.
  ISBN 0-395-59506-1
  [1. Missing persons — Fiction. 2. New Mexico — Fiction. 3. Mexican
Americans — Fiction. 4. Mystery and detective stories.] I. Title.
PZ7.M478150n 1992   91-12864
[Fic] — dc20   CIP
                  AC

"Nothing Gold Can Stay," by Robert Frost,
from THE POETRY OF ROBERT FROST edited by
Edward Connery Lathem. Copyright 1923, © 1969
by Holt, Rinehart and Winston, copyright 1951 by
Robert Frost. Reprinted by permission of
Henry Holt and Company, Inc.

Printed in the United States of America

HAD 10 9 8 7 6 5 4 3 2 1

For Walt and Lil

I'd like to acknowledge the advice and encouragement of my friends. Thank you, Lois Trembly, Kate Keely, and Tony Rosado. And thanks, also, to a gentle editor, Matilda W. Welter.

The One Who Came Back

• • • Chapter One

IN BOLD LETTERS gouged into two unpainted boards, the sign said:

SANDIA MTN. TRAPPERS
& GOLD-MINING CO.

The sign, nailed high on the trunk of an old fir tree, was hidden by the drooping branches.

The two partners knew it was there. If they wanted to look, they could see it from where they worked by the edge of the stream.

Their heads bent over the shallow pan that Alex Grant moved back and forth. His hair was a cinnamon-colored shock, as stubborn in its direction as straws in a whiskbroom. Eddie Chavez's black hair was softer, hanging shaggy over his forehead.

The rhythmic motion of the pan sloshed wavelets of water over the edge. Left behind was a residue of black sand caught in the riffles in the bottom of the pan. Staring intently at the silty paste, they thought they saw their futures in it.

1

Eddie's black eyes shone with excitement. He held a thin paintbrush, not as thick as a pencil, and tried to stab it into the residue.

"Hey, man, hold still. There's one. I see it." Eddie's voice bubbled out, excited but not loud. Even when Eddie yelled, his voice had a plaintive, faraway sound to it.

"Hold on, Eddie. I think there's more than one. Let me wash some more of this crud out of here."

Alex dipped more water from the basin he and Eddie had scooped at the edge of the stream. His rough, red hands held the pan steady so he wouldn't lose any of the silt as he dipped it under water. Back and forth he rocked it. With each motion, the muddy water surged over the lip, carrying with it some of the lighter sand.

"You're gonna throw it out," Eddie complained.

"No, I'm not. Gold is heavier than anything else in that pan. It doesn't float. You know that. Now look." Alex poked in the shimmery film in the bottom of the pan and started to grin. "I see three," he said.

"Yeah, man. Hold still." Eddie steadied the pan. Carefully he dipped the brush at the show of gold flake. The brush hairs caught and lifted the raggedy-edged bit of metal. Holding the small dot so they both could admire it, Eddie smiled hugely.

Alex took a glass vial from his shirt-pocket and unscrewed the top. The tiny bottle contained a drop of muddy water and four flecks that Alex was pretty sure were gold.

Panning for gold was probably easier if you learned

it from someone who knew how. He and Pop had never panned, but Pop had bought the little vials for him. All but this one still sat on his bureau unused.

As much as he studied the encyclopedia and the old books in the library, Alex was not sure if he was swirling the pan right. It was hard to learn from printed words. He knew there were secrets to looking for the deep hidden places where gold might be waiting after it washed down the arroyo. It seemed that the back-breaking work they did ought to produce more than these few confetti-sized pieces of the precious metal.

"How many of these dots does it take to make an ounce?" Eddie asked, as he had many times before.

"Oh, maybe a thousand," Alex said. His answer never varied.

"We need a better place to dig."

"Maybe in the spring. It's getting too cold up here to do much more panning this winter. I'm cold now. Aren't you?"

"Naw," Eddie said. Both of them had wet shoes and pant legs from kneeling in the damp sand. Their sleeves were wet to the shoulder.

Alex Grant was the bulkier of the two, with more growth still pushing through him. Eddie Chavez was a contrast to Alex in every way. Black eyes danced in an open face. Alex's eyes were pale and his face guarded. Eddie's amber skin seemed suited to every extreme of New Mexico weather. Alex's light skin reddened, roughened, and peeled whether it was winter or summer.

3

"Let's clear up here and then eat lunch, OK?"

With the small shovel, Alex filled the scooped-out hole where they had dipped the pan. He raked out the mound of discarded gravel and sand. Finally, the stream ran clear again. Alex was orderly. He liked an orderly life. He even liked nature to be orderly.

When he finished working, Alex hurried to pull on his padded vest and button it across his heavy canvas shirt.

The November sky darkened. Overhead, clouds scudded in front of the sun and tumbled toward the mountains like dust balls escaping from under a bed. The wind flipped the tops of the ponderosas and riffled through their lower branches. The aspen trees were almost bare, the fallen leaves still golden. Even in this protected fold of the Sandia Mountains that he and Eddie called The Flats, Alex could feel the wind.

There would be snow before long, he knew. Alex was a child of the desert. Born in New Mexico, he had lived all his fifteen years here. He could smell moisture, anticipate snow. The promise of it teased at tomorrow.

Alex dragged satisfying gulps of air into his chest. Sometimes, in his life down below, he felt he couldn't breathe.

The whine of a jet razored through the air as it rose from Kirtland Air Force Base. The high-pitched tone sharpened an anxiety in Alex.

"Come on," he said gruffly to Eddie. "We'd better eat."

· · ·

The sun was out again as they sat amidst an outcrop of granite boulders. From here, they looked three or four thousand feet down on the sprawl of Albuquerque. The western horizon, studded with dead volcano cones, seemed to generate clouds. These spread across the Rio Grande Valley, casting dark shadows across some neighborhoods. Other streets were picked out for momentary stardom as the sun's rays hit them like a giant spotlight.

Eddie finished his sandwich. Holding the vial up, he rocked it until several bits of metal clung to the sides.

"What do you think? How much is this worth?" Eddie asked.

"It was over three hundred dollars an ounce the last time I looked," Alex said. He had tried to get Eddie to come with him to the school library so they could look the price up in the newspaper. Eddie was shy about going to places that were new to him.

"It'll take a while to make any money this way. Maybe we can run a trapline up here this winter. Maybe take some foxes, huh?"

"Yeah, maybe," Alex said. He remembered their one botched try at trapping.

"Well, I know how I'm going to spend mine," Eddie said. They had planned the spending so much that it unreeled like a tape. Still, there were details to be worked on.

"First the house for Mom. Paid for. All paid for, so she can kick Paco out." This was the formula with which Eddie always started. Today, the mention of Paco made Alex's eyes slide to Eddie's face. The shadow of a bruise still stained the brown skin under his right eye.

No less generous, Alex would rent an apartment for his mother, Boots. He couldn't see her as being domestic enough for a house. She had really liked living in Gabe's condo that time when Alex was little and came to visit her. Then — he never said it out loud, but nursed it in his own mind — he'd somehow fix up Mom and Pop's situation so he could live with them again. Alex missed his grandparents so much; he didn't think about it because of the hurt.

"Then," Eddie continued, "a good lawyer to get Johnny out of the pen in Texas." Eddie's voice always got whispery and dry when he talked about his big brother.

With these obligations taken care of, the two turned to their personal dreams. For Eddie, a Harley-Davidson and probably a 'Vette. He even carried a magazine in his backpack so he could study the details of various models.

Alex had to have something with a four-wheel drive. His future depended on getting as far from civilization as he could. He'd need horses, maybe mules.

Today, as he did most days, he also remembered his mother's need for a new car. "I think I'll get one of those Nissan Sentras for Boots. What do you think?"

6

"Better than that gas-hog she's got now. What year is it?" Eddie asked.

"I'm not sure. When I was a little kid and she drove to Cruces to see us, the Maverick was old then. It had a bumper sticker that said Don't Laugh. It's Paid For."

Eddie laughed. He jumped up and climbed to the top of a boulder. In Eddie, mind and body both kept jumping from one thing to another. "I can see the high school from here," he said. "I wonder if they missed us today."

"Maybe. Lots of kids ditch on Friday. We'll probably get called to the counselor's office on Monday." The anxiety that nudged at Alex when he heard the jet gave him twinges again. He had never ditched school before today. He didn't really know what to expect. In fact, in his eight years of school, and the beginning of this ninth year, he had pretty much escaped the attention of the front office. Here, in Albuquerque, at Canyon High, he sometimes thought the teachers didn't even know when he was in class.

"This is lots better than the cafeteria, isn't it?" Alex asked.

"Yeah, and better than math, and better than the stupid assembly this afternoon. Who wants to see the jocks? Who cares about the big football game?"

"I like to watch the cheerleaders."

"Yeah. The chicks. I like to watch Audrey and Liz in Careers class. Those uniforms kill me. When they walk, the skirts are like Venetian blinds moving across their butts. All black, then flip, and you see gold streaks."

Alex smiled. There was a glossiness about the cheer-leaders, as though they were packaged in shrink wrap. His eyes always followed them on the days when they wore their uniforms. There were other girls like them in his classes, too.

But in English class, he found his attention more and more drawn to Gwen. With her crazy hats, which she wore like a trademark, and her loose-fitting jumpers, Gwen attracted by her very demureness.

After a silence, Eddie said, "I wish Candy could come up here with us." He peeled an orange with deft fingers.

"Yeah, he's cool. Let's call him when we get back. Tell him how we ditched today to come to the mountains."

"OK. He might be little, but he's better than guys twice his size."

"What did you say is wrong with him?" Alex asked.

"Something wrong with his bones. I don't know what the name is. His bones break real easy. Like toothpicks. Then they don't grow right."

Ditching school to come to their special place in the mountains had made Eddie feel better. Alex tried to weigh that fact against his own anxiety about getting into trouble.

· · ·

That morning when he had stopped by Eddie's trailer to pick him up for the walk to the bus stop, Eddie was subdued. He wouldn't look Alex in the eye. A swelled lump on his cheekbone was still red.

"What happened?" Alex asked.

"Oh, nothing," Eddie said, trying to be cool. He felt the bruise with a gentle finger. "Paco decked me, is all."

Paco was Eddie's stepfather. Alex could hear him sometimes, slamming doors and yelling in their trailer next door to the one where Alex and his mother lived.

Eddie looked so sad that Alex wanted to help him claim some bravado. He asked, "Did you hit him back?"

"Naw. My mom was there. She took up for him. Told me to stay out of his way. She thinks we need his paycheck, but he drinks up most of it. We got along OK after my dad got killed. Even after the narcs got Johnny. We don't need Paco Rodriguez."

Alex knew Eddie's mother worked in Albertson's bakery and the kids got Social Security because their dad was gone. Alex and Boots didn't get anything from Alex's father. They didn't even talk about him.

The two boys walked slowly toward their bus stop on Indian School Road. "I'm just gonna leave, just split," Eddie muttered.

"Yeah." The idea of running away had crossed Alex's mind, too.

"Let's ditch today," Eddie said in his whispery voice.

Alex hesitated for a moment. Then he agreed. "Yeah, they'll never miss us. They've got too many kids there already." Without another word, they knew what they would do on their day off.

To avoid being seen by any of Eddie's family, they

sneaked back to the trailer court. In the trailer that was Alex's home, Boots slept in the bedroom at the end of the narrow hall. She wouldn't awaken until ten or eleven o'clock. She'd never know they had returned here without going to school.

They got the supplies they needed from Alex's kitchen. Alex lent Eddie an old rucksack.

Eddie watched the door to his own home. When the last of his brothers left, he slipped out the door and ran, doubled up, to the laundry building. When he came back, he held his hand over something tucked into the waistband of his pants. Inside Alex's kitchen, he pulled out a small, dull-gray automatic.

"Where'd you get that?"

"It's Paco's," Eddie explained. He looked triumphant, as though he'd put one over on his stepfather. "He is mean when he gets drunk. He might shoot someone, so I swiped it. I hid it under the laundry building. Maybe we'll see something to shoot today."

"That gun's not for shooting animals. It's too little. Besides, you don't have bullets."

"Sure I do," Eddie said. He brought a small box from his pocket and put it on the counter. Holding back the catch on the butt of the gun, he started to pull out the clip.

"Don't load it here," Alex said. "Just put it in that day pack and we'll take it with us."

Eddie's excitement died down. After wrapping the gun and box in his nylon jacket, he placed the bundle carefully in the bottom of the pack.

"Is that why Paco decked you? Because you took his gun?" Alex asked.

"Naw. He doesn't even know I've got it. He hit me because I smarted off to him."

• • •

On their bikes, they pumped up the long slope toward the mountains, past shopping centers, apartment complexes, and acres of houses. They felt conspicuous on their big-tired kid bikes. There weren't any other kids on the streets. The school buses had swung through the neighborhoods, clearing the corners of clumps of waiting children.

Alex and Eddie kept their eyes on the mountains. Looking remote and unattainable, the Sandias rose in blue layers to the jagged crest. They gave no clue that they concealed the world of the Sandia Mtn. Trappers & Gold-Mining Co.

At the edge of the Cibola National Forest, they left their bikes and went up Embudito Canyon. Like a gnarled finger, the canyon poked and prodded up the mountainside. At first, the canyon was desert-dry. Then, crowded with willows and the fallen bodies of old cottonwoods, the canyon pushed higher into ponderosas and Douglas firs. About two thirds of the way to the crest, the canyon flattened out to hold the area the boys called The Flats.

They had come here every Saturday and Sunday since they met in August. Here they forgot the humiliation of having to ride kid bikes. They forgot the

Belvedere Heights Trailer Court. They forgot Canyon High School. The world on this mountainside was more real than any part of their weekday life in Albuquerque.

. . .

"Aren't you cold, Eddie?" Alex asked again as he saw the wind stir Eddie's hair.

Eddie jumped down and shoved his amber-colored arm out at Alex. "Look. No goose bumps." His black pants and short-sleeved black T-shirt was almost a uniform. Only the messages changed. This faded shirt, tight across Eddie's angular shoulders, celebrated a long-ago Metallica concert.

"Hey, man, you're always thinking," Eddie said. He couldn't stay quiet for long. He jumped to another boulder.

"I was just thinking what a great place this is. And it's all ours." Alex grinned. With the rustling, creaking tree noises, the leaf mold smell, the sun drying out his clothes, and his anxiety pushed to the back of his mind, he was content.

"I'll bet no one comes up here on weekdays," Alex said.

"People who do come stay on the trail. Afraid of getting lost, I guess." Eddie laughed.

There were signs that the official trail had once run through here. One of the older ponderosas was scarred by a blaze cut long ago. A shelter — just half-logs making one side and a roof overhang — was rotting

12

and covered with moss. Rocks blackened by old fires lay about.

In staking their claim to The Flats, Eddie and Alex buried ashes and carried away bottles, Spam cans, and wads of plastic.

The woods where he was going to live would be denser, Alex thought, not so tame-looking as these. He wouldn't have to carry in water. The water that ran through his future place would be pure. Not contaminated by people or livestock. There would be game for food and trapping.

Alex lay back against the granite, enchanted by his future. The smell of the pine duff under him was intoxicating. He looked at the sky, still turquoise in patches. The sun-sparkled whorls of ponderosa needles hypnotized him.

. . .

"Hey, Alex, don't go to sleep." Eddie stood over him, black eyes kinetic with energy and fun. His skin was satiny, the color of varnish. Already his cheeks had black down and his upper lip had a definite mustache. He was going to let it grow to a Fu Manchu, Eddie said. He'd wear dark glasses and look like the cartoons of a Chicano on the walls of the boys' restroom at the high school.

"I'm gonna hide and you find me." Eddie's face was split by a huge grin. Alex loved to see him smile, see how his teeth glistened with spit. Eddie side-skipped away, watching for a response.

"The sun's getting low. We can't stay up here much longer," Alex said. Then foreseeing Eddie's resistance, Alex added, "I've got to get home before Boots leaves for work or I'll be in trouble." This wasn't true. It was a fiction he maintained, even with Eddie. When he moved in with Boots in August, she didn't know how to be a mother. Only once in a while did she remember that she was responsible for him. Alex was trying to coach Boots into accountability.

"It's not that late. It's just that we don't have daylight saving now." That was the way Eddie reasoned. Alex was used to it and didn't try to get him to explain what he was thinking.

"Eddie, look at those clouds. And the wind's picking up. There's a storm coming in. We don't have time," Alex said. He raised himself on his elbow to watch Eddie edge away.

"Just once. I'm gonna hide. Betcha can't find me."

He danced off, turning to look back at Alex. His feet crashed through the floor of leaves, exploding clouds of leaf dust to hang golden in the air. Next to a grove of aspens, Eddie jumped high before he took off. For an instant, he was suspended, a black figure against the pale trunks. The few leaves still on the trees made a tattered halo against the sky.

• • • Chapter Two

ALEX PICKED UP the wads of plastic wrap and the juice cartons and put them in his day pack. In the outside pocket, he stuck the almost empty flask of water. Over the back he fastened the GI shovel and black mining pan. It had been some time since he heard Eddie's footsteps in the noisy leaves. "Let him wait awhile," Alex thought. "Maybe he'll get impatient and come back to see why I'm not looking for him."

He cinched the last strap on his pack and stashed it inside the lean-to. Eddie was still not back. Alex would have to play his game.

In a grim frame of mind, he checked Eddie's usual hiding places. The huddle of stunted oaks beyond the aspens, the cavity under the big boulders near where they ate lunch, the overhanging branches of the big fir tree. Nothing. No sign of him.

Away from the shelter of the rock outcropping, the wind whipped branches across the trail. Alex zipped

15

his jacket. His shoes and the bottom of his pants' legs weren't dry yet. They were cold. He trotted up the trail where he last heard Eddie. Eddie was fast and could be sneaky.

Leaving The Flats, he headed up the mountain on the old trail. It was steep and narrow, in places only as wide as his foot. Alex and Eddie rarely came up here. On the right, it fell off, straight down, so a hiker was looking into the tops of spruce trees. Farther up, the trail ran across a stretch of scree. The barren field of loose rock started high on the upside of the trail and sprawled below the trail for one hundred or so steep feet until it ran against a border of stunted oaks and juniper. No place to hide on either side of the trail here.

Alex turned back down the mountain, loping now. He scrambled down the bank of the arroyo where it widened into the stream that went through The Flats. Twisting through underbrush and splashing through the water, he plunged like a hound looking for a scent.

Finally, he gave that up and went back upstream to the lean-to. "Eddie isn't playing a simple hide-and-seek game," Alex thought. "He's playing ambush or stalking."

"Eddie," he yelled, "quit fooling around. We've got to go." Only the singing wind answered. Frustrated, he screeched, "Eddie, damn you, come on."

Feeling self-conscious, knowing that Eddie might be hiding right now watching his anger mount, Alex got ready to go home. At the lean-to, he got his own pack and slipped into the shoulder straps. Back by the

16

outcropping, he gathered up Eddie's jacket and old aluminum cup and stuffed them into Eddie's pack.

The weight of Eddie's pack surprised him until he remembered the gun in the bottom. Before they started panning, they had polished the gun. Eddie showed Alex how to load it and they pinged at a piece of paper stuck onto a stub of a branch. After each took a round, they were disappointed to find the gun wasn't accurate unless they stood close to the target.

"I'm glad I'm not trying to hit a rattlesnake," Eddie said.

"Yeah, it's not much good in the woods, is it?" Alex agreed.

Alex made sure the clip was out and the chamber empty. He wrapped the gun in Eddie's jacket and replaced it in the pack.

He strapped Eddie's pack across his chest. If Eddie was watching, this might make him feel possessive and come out of hiding to snatch the pack away. Alex stopped rustling the nylon packs and stood quietly to listen. Except for the wind lashing the tops of the trees, there was no sound.

Once more he yelled, "I'm going home now. I'm going home. Just stay here if you want to."

On the way down the mountain, he stayed with the arroyo, which opened out to become Embudito Canyon. He could only think that Eddie had hidden somewhere on this route waiting for Alex to come down. So he watched, tensed for Eddie's spring from behind a boulder.

Alex seethed. First he hadn't found Eddie in the

usual places. Then he had to carry all their equipment. He knew that his anger would only add to Eddie's enjoyment of his joke. A dumb joke — to lie in ambush and try to scare him.

Alex could almost hear him. "Hey, man. Why're you ticked off? It's no big deal." Alex could even imagine his whispery laugh. Eddie was always scoffing at Alex's concern about dangers in the mountains — things like rock slides and hypothermia. "Big deal," Eddie would say.

But Eddie didn't have much experience in the outdoors. In August when he and Alex had come up here for the first time, Eddie had talked about bears and snakes. Now, after their trips this fall, he was too confident. He refused to think that the weather could turn dangerous.

By the time Alex worked his way down to the mouth of the canyon, the air was filled with swirling clouds of snow. At the very last good pool of water in the canyon, Alex smelled smoke before he saw two people huddled over a fire. The visibility was so bad, Alex could see only what they weren't. They weren't Eddie. He skirted around them as he crashed through willow thickets where Eddie might hide.

The snow stopped. Looking out over the city, he could see narrow beams of sunlight breaking through the cloud cover. Pop always said you could have any kind of weather you wanted in New Mexico. It often snowed in the mountains, while the city at their feet went about sun-filled desert activities. Alex was covered with a wet film when he reached the rusted-out car body where they had hidden their bikes this morning. His battered Raleigh was there. But Eddie's bike was gone.

"That bastard," Alex thought. "Why did he go home without me? What got into him?"

The wind whipped cutting sand into Alex's face. He jerked his bike onto the packed dirt road and hurtled down the canyon onto paved streets.

Alex chewed it over. "Why would Eddie leave?" His pants' legs felt like frozen tubes of ice. Even with his camouflage shirt buttoned tight and his quilted vest zipped to his chin, he was rigid with cold. Maybe Eddie, in his short sleeves, was just too cold to wait. He hightailed it home. He'd be waiting there, warm and dry, ready to jeer at Alex.

•   •   •

At the trailer court, Alex saw that Boots's green Maverick was gone. He'd spent so much time looking for Eddie that he'd missed her. He wondered if she'd noticed that he wasn't home yet.

He started for Eddie's trailer. But Paco Rodriguez's beat-up truck was parked there. He changed his direction and went down to the end of the dirt street to the laundry building. On the lee side of the faded-green prefab stood Eddie's sister, Deenie, with some younger kids. Her black pants were skintight as she bent over with a large cosmetic brush to paint the cheek of mop-headed ten-year-old Angela.

Deenie was fourteen, as tall as Alex, but thin. Her dark brown hair was cut in a straight line all the way around her head. It curved forward in loose crescents toward each cheek. Her eyes looked from behind bangs that moved in separate fringes. When Deenie looked at him, Alex felt uneasy, as though he was going to break into a sweat. When he tried to return her flirting stare, his look was drawn to her eyelids. Her black make-up made her look like a cocker spaniel.

Deenie straightened up, shot her thin hip out toward Alex, and looked at his muddy clothes.

"Hey, Redhead. You and Eddie didn't go to school today, did you? Stella said she didn't see you on the bus."

"Deenie, where is Eddie?" Alex felt his throat tightening. Sometimes when he talked with girls he felt he was going to strangle.

"Don't you know? Where'd you guys go? Did you go to the mall? To Winrock?" She tossed her head and made the short drapery of hair move across her forehead.

"We went up on the mountain. But Eddie ran off and left me. Have you seen him?" Alex's throat was closing and the question rasped out.

"No. I didn't see him. What do you guys do up there, huh? Play cowboys and Indians?" She giggled and glanced at her attendants to be sure they shared her wit.

"Cut it out, Deenie. I've gotta find Eddie."

"Be that way, Redhead." Dennie flipped her other hip and dismissed Alex from her presence.

At the beginning of the dirt street, down by the

entrance, a double-wide trailer commanded the Belvedere Heights Trailer Court. This was the home of the Endicotts, the manager-couple, also suspected of being the owners. Ten trailers lined the rutted dirt street, five on each side. All alike, they were so old nobody even thought of the nicer-sounding "mobile home" to describe them. The kitchen end of each trailer pointed to the street. A door opened into the kitchen from rickety stoops. Farther back along the side was another door. In most of the trailers it was unused and had no steps leading to it.

Alex went to Eddie's trailer and knocked on the kitchen door.

From inside, Alex heard the TV. He wished Eddie's mother were home, but knew she was still at work. Bobby opened the door. Light flooded across the stoop. TV noise rushed out around him.

"Is Eddie here?" Alex raised his voice so Bobby could hear him over the blare of the TV.

"Who is that, Bobby?" Paco yelled. Heavy footsteps. The door crashed wide open. Bobby ducked out of the way. Alex was face to face with Paco Rodriguez.

"Do you know where Eddie is?" Alex asked.

Eddie's stepfather held the door wide open, oblivious of the wind whipping scraps of sand at him. His feet were bare, his pants were unfastened at the waistband, and his belly spilled over. He was only a little taller than Alex, but his heavy arms and big shoulders spoke of strength.

"What do you mean, 'Where's Eddie?' You guys didn't go to school today. Where've you been?"

21

"On the mountain. But Eddie came down first. I don't know where he is."

"You're lying," Paco Rodriguez said. His breath hit Alex's face in beery gusts. His eyes narrowed down to red-rimmed slits. "You guys are up to something, aren't you? You've cooked up something. Eddie's run away, hasn't he?"

"I told you . . ." Alex started to say, but ducked back as Paco Rodriguez shot out a hand to grab his shirtfront. The boy jumped off the stoop and scrambled for his own trailer. He was relieved to hear the door slam closed behind Rodriguez.

• • •

Alex didn't know what to do. He needed an adult, someone to say, "This is serious. We'll call the police." Or maybe they'd say, "Don't worry. Eddie will show up."

"Stupid Eddie. Stupid Alex, too, I guess," Alex thought.

There was Boots, his mother. He needed to let her know he was home. He'd call her at work and ask her what to do, but he already knew. She'd say, "Don't worry. Everything is going to be all right."

Many days he didn't see her or talk to her for more than fifteen minutes. When he came home from school, she said, "Bye, sweets," and drove off in her junker that trailed its stream of oily smoke. She came home from work at two or three in the morning and was sleeping when he left for school. Out of this schedule, he had been trying to shape the kind of life he had with Mom and Pop.

With them, growing up wasn't so abrupt. One year flowed into another and each year there was more liberty, more responsibility. Here, it was all liberty, all responsibility. From here, adulthood didn't look like anything he wanted to rush into.

Liz, the cashier, answered when Alex called the Capital J Bar. She called him sweetie and said Boots hadn't come in yet, but she'd tell her that Alex had called.

Slipping outside quietly, Alex went to the back of Eddie's trailer. The slot between the trailer and the cinder-block wall where Eddie kept his bike was empty.

"I sure wish I could call Pop and ask him what to do." Alex picked up the phone but put it down. He wasn't supposed to call long-distance. Pop and Mom always called on Sunday from their new home in Arizona.

Alex fought not to give in to a little-kid feeling of helplessness. He had told Paco Rodriguez that they were on the mountain and that Eddie hadn't come back with Alex. So one adult knew. Eddie's mother would know when she got home from work. They could decide if it was serious enough to call the police.

He was hungry. Standing in front of the open refrigerator, he analyzed his possibilities. Food didn't occupy a place of great importance in the trailer. Not as an everyday thing. Sometimes, Boots got interested.

23

Her enthusiasms rose and fell in such bewildering extremes that Alex often forgot what belief they were living that week. Sometimes, it was no dairy products, then no beef. Then no chicken, or apples. Now there were boxes of Tiger's Milk sitting in the cupboard, and leftover pizza and diet Cokes in the refrigerator. Alex ate the pizza.

He switched on the TV and switched it off again. He turned on the tap in the kitchen to get a drink of water. He turned off the tap when he couldn't remember why he was there. A feeling was growing in him.

"Eddie's not joking around. If Eddie plays a trick, he wants to see the payoff fast," Alex thought. Eddie wouldn't wait until sometime late in the evening and show up saying, "Ha, ha, were you worried about me?" That was not his style of joke.

"Besides," Alex reasoned, "he doesn't have anyplace to hang out. He doesn't have friends here in the Heights, except for me. Eddie wouldn't just hang out by himself at some video place or something. He's not a loner.

"He doesn't like to be alone." That thought jolted Alex. Eddie was still on the mountain. He was injured. That's why he hadn't come down. Too badly injured to reply when Alex called. In his hasty search, Alex had been expecting Eddie to jump out at him. He had not looked for a body lying quietly at the base of some big boulders.

Now. He knew what to do. Get out his big framed backpack. Put stuff in: his sleeping bag, water, crackers. He scuffled through the cabinet shelves looking for something sweet. He pulled out a small jar of jam and a box of Jell-O. Eddie would need some fast calories if he was injured and had to spend a cold night up there. He got his parka from the closet in his room. A note for Boots, even though he'd probably be back before she got home. Yeah, and a flashlight. Matches. If he were out there for very long, he'd need something to eat himself. An apple and a slab of cheese from the refrigerator. He sure needed to shop tomorrow. There wasn't much here.

Careful. He'd have to be careful all the way. Take the bike trail up by the flood ditch. Avoid the evening traffic. His bike didn't have lights, just big round reflectors on the spokes.

The books — the ones he studied about backpacking and mountaineering — said not to try to travel in the mountains at night and never to go alone. "But if it's an emergency," Alex thought, "you have to break the rules."

• • • Chapter Three

THE HEAVY POLICE CAR left the dirt road and bounced across rocks and hummocks of grama grass. The strong rays of the headlights lapped in waves across the sandy mouth of Embudito Canyon. Alex crouched in the back seat of the police car, inside a cage like the one of the dogcatcher's truck. Tension made him tremble as he tried to guide the Mexican driver to the spot where he and Eddie had left their bicycles that morning. Could he have lost his way in the strangeness of this night world? He had never been here in a car or at night.

In a way, he was relieved that the police had picked him up. He wasn't surprised that they knew his name. As he guessed, Eddie's mother had called the police as soon as she got home. And Bobby probably saw him leave the trailer court with the backpack. Bobby would know that the backpack meant Alex was going to the mountains.

Slowly the wave of light washed over the willows

and the rusted car body lying on its side at the far edge of the canyon mouth. When they were bumper-close to the rusted carcass, they stopped. The light bleached the metal and the willows into whiteness against the swallowing darkness beyond.

Alex groped for a handle to the door. There was no inside handle, no way out of the cage. The Anglo policeman put his cap on, got out of the car, and opened the back door from the outside. Alex climbed over the backpack he had braced against the back seat. The Mexican driver stayed behind the wheel. Either he was bored or he was very good at faking it.

"This is it, huh? This is the right place?" the Anglo officer asked.

Alex didn't answer but started toward the deep shadow between the wreck and the willows. The officer laid a hand on his upper arm and Alex waited while he rummaged under the front seat and found a large flashlight, the kind Alex and his grandfather used to take camping. He stepped in front of Alex and shined the light into the hiding place, then let it illuminate the ground. Heavy shadows showed the snake-like trails left by bicycle tires. But they were indented by shoe prints. Alex stretched his arms out and leaned forward as though trying to conjure up a legible record, the written story of the bicycles.

The policeman had his back to the car lights, which fell full on Alex's face. Dismay registered on his broad, white face and his guarded eyes opened wide.

"Are you sure this is the place, son?" the officer asked.

"Yes, right here. I thought there'd be tracks so I could see if Eddie got his bike."

"Well, I'd say I saw the tracks of two bikes in here. Lots of footprints, though. What kind of shoes were you wearing? Those?"

He shined the light at Alex's feet and Alex turned his foot up to show him the tread on his sneakers.

"Do you remember the kind of shoes Eddie has on?" he asked.

Alex remembered and clamped his lips shut. Everything he said just added to the confusion. Finally he muttered, "Reeboks, just like mine, but older."

Alex stared intently at the smudged tracks. "There," he said, "there's a small print, smooth sole. There's another, broader. On top of the bike tracks. They come over from those houses over there." Alex pointed to the housing development that climbed the foothills to the south of Embudito Canyon. "Kids. Little kids come over here."

"Well, we can't follow those tracks. The wind has wiped out everything except the marks on this side of the car body."

The policeman led Alex back to the car. The Mexican partner turned off the engine and got out to stand beside Alex. Silently, Alex and the Mexican cop watched the moving pattern of light from the flashlight lace through the willows. The Anglo returned to the car and positioned the light so Alex's face was well lit. The Mexican officer got a jacket from the car, and the snicker of the zipper made Alex think of some night-bird sound. The other officer took a small note-book and pen from his pocket.

"Nothing," the policeman said.

For a moment they were all silent, a little tableau. The Sandia Mountains loomed in back of them, dense and dark. Albuquerque spread out below like a jew-eled tapestry on a loom. It was pulled along the Rio Grande Valley to the north and south, and stretched to the western horizon by the shuttles of car lights weaving on the interstate highways. A cloud cover hung ragged, making a low ceiling over the city and pressing down over the crest of the mountains.

The police radio crackled softly. A jet from Kirtland Air Force Base whined in a sharp climb. Embudito Canyon sucked the last of the warm November air up the slopes of the forbidding mountain, leaving cold eddies swirling around the group.

"Well, Alex, you been leading us on a wild goose chase?" the Anglo asked softly.

There was times when Alex couldn't put words to his thoughts, when they roiled and tumbled in his head. No thoughts came. He stubbornly repeated what he knew.

"We left our bikes here this morning. This after-noon when I came down, Eddie's bike was gone. I thought he went home. But when I got to the trailer court, he wasn't there. So I came back to look for him."

Alex heard the radio in the car crackle. With his hands dug deep into the slash pockets of his jacket, he motioned with an elbow. "Can you call his home on that thing? See if Eddie's there yet."

"Pete?" the Anglo asked.

The Mexican went to the driver's side of the car and talked into the mike. They could hear the dispatcher mumbling through some directory, looking for the number of the Francisco Rodriguez who lived in the Belvedere Heights Trailer Court near Indian School Road. With some coaching from Pete, she found it and called. Over the speaker they heard her voice crackle, "No. Eddie Chavez is not at home. They haven't heard from him."

"So, where is Eddie? Did he get his bike and ride to a friend's house?" The Anglo talked softly but leaned toward Alex.

"No. If he had his bike and rode anywhere, he'd go home. He'd find me," Alex said. "He's still up there. He's hurt or something." Despite his words, Alex was not sure. These policemen — they were supposed to know about these things. After he had told them what he knew, the were supposed to know where Eddie was, whether he was lost or not. They always knew on TV.

"Tell me again what you did when you got home and found Eddie wasn't there. Did you tell anyone?" the officer asked.

In the dim light, Alex could see his white badge. It said R. Marlow. The boy was glad he had noticed the name. "Marlow" was better than "the Anglo." "Pete" was better than "the Mexican." In school, in New Mexico history, they made a big deal about the three cultures in the state. But Alex didn't like to think of people with labels. That was too much like talking about dogs — that beagle, that collie.

"Yes, sir. When I went to Eddie's trailer to find out if he was there. I told Eddie's dad — stepfather, really — that Eddie didn't come off the mountain with me. Eddie's mother called you guys, didn't she?"

Alex's face prickled as though the light were causing some sort of rash on him. He didn't say anything about Paco Rodriguez smelling of beer and trying to grab him. Eddie was Alex's friend and Alex wasn't going to trash his family, not even his stepdad.

"And then," Marlow prodded.

Alex's voice came dry and harsh. "I packed some food. Cheese and stuff and water. My old sleeping bag. Then I got on my bike and started toward Embudito. You guys picked me up before I got past Juan Tabo Road."

"Why, Alex? Where were you taking this stuff?"

"I'm taking it in case I find Eddie and he's hurt. He can freeze to death up there tonight unless I find him. It's gonna be cold. Maybe snow."

"But it's dark, Alex. How can you see?"

"I know. I know. The books say . . . But I've got a flashlight and I know the canyon pretty well. Eddie and me, we've been coming up here every weekend since the beginning of August."

"If you thought Eddie was lying up there injured, why didn't you call the police? We could get search and rescue teams with trained dogs. Why didn't you call us?"

"I'm not a grown-up. I didn't know what to do." Alex looked at the mountain — at its unyielding blackness. Even if a search team couldn't see much at night, the dogs could pick up a trail.

"That's a good idea," he said. "Can't you do it now? Call the search team. It's not too late. Not too cold yet. I can go with them, show them where I saw Eddie last." Alex felt hopeful. Maybe he could put this awful question of what to do, what to think, in the hands of an adult. An official adult — the police.

"We want to be sure there's someone up there to search for. Getting all those people out here, with the lights and equipment and dogs. That's a lot of trouble." Marlow was quiet. A long silence. The wind whipped a tumbleweed past their legs. It danced out of the car lights toward the arroyo. Silence. Maybe the policeman thought the silence would squeeze something from Alex. Some blurted-out thing about where Eddie really was.

Alex felt the pressure. The question of what to do was laid on him again. He wanted to say something so convincing that they would have to search for Eddie.

"I know he's up there. He's hurt and can't walk or he'd come down. We've got to find him and help him." Alex's voice went into a little kid's whine and then ended on a falsetto that he hated to hear.

"Do you really know where Eddie is, Alex? Right now, do you know where to find him?"

"No, but I could look. I could show someone where we were, where he might be," Alex said urgently. He tried to talk low so that he could keep control of his voice. No wonder the police weren't convinced. How could he expect to impress them if his voice kept sliding out from under him?

The radio crackled some numbers. Pete went around to the driver's side and spoke into the mike. Alex wasn't sure what it was about. The call seemed to speed up both policemen as though they had to make a decision and move on, had to finish this and be somewhere else.

"Alex, I'm gonna make a guess," Marlow said. He had his hand on Alex's shoulder. Gently, but insistently, he pushed him against the side of the car. "You know exactly where Eddie is. And he's not up there. He's got his bike and he's hiding someplace. In a culvert or a flood ditch. You're taking him food and a sleeping bag. Tell me where you're supposed to meet him."

"No. I'm not. He's up there, I tell you. He's gotta be up there. And he's going to die if I don't go help him." Alex's voice cracked again, and the skin around his eyes stiffened as he tried to keep from crying. He wished he were grown-up and could push this guy against the car and make him understand.

"Let's look at that pack. See if you thought to put in a first-aid kit or something like that." Marlow turned on a light inside the car and pulled the old, smoke-soaked sleeping bag from the backpack. The ends of its tangled strings brought up a sweater. Then he found the flashlight, the food packet, and water. From the very bottom, he pulled out a hot-rod magazine. On the cover, a black-haired woman was sprawled across the hood of a car. Her inviting look, her too-small bra, and her high-cut shorts didn't seem to have a lot to do with the contents of the magazine.

Marlow held the magazine right under Alex's nose until the boy breathed in the ink and turned red. "I suppose if Eddie can't watch TV he has to have some entertainment."

"That was in there from before. I didn't put it in there this evening. Honest. You're trying to stack things to look like I'm lying. I'm trying to tell you . . ."

Marlow stuffed the gear into the backpack and motioned Alex into the back seat. Locked in that cage, Alex yelled — louder and more belligerently than he intended. "Let me out. I can find Eddie by myself."

"Let's just not deliver any food or warm sweaters to Eddie and see how long he stays away. He's going to get cold and hungry and he's going to come home."

"You can't make me go home," Alex yelled.

"Sure we can. You've broken the curfew law. You're only fifteen years old — not old enough to be out alone this time of night."

Alex leaned back and muttered to himself, "Curfew law. I'll bet he's just making that up." As he quieted down, he thought, "Maybe they're right. They wouldn't leave a kid up on the mountain to freeze to death. They probably investigate kids every day who don't come home. Who run away. Split. That was what Eddie said this morning. Said he was going to split. He could be someplace warm now. At some relative's house, laughing that funny laugh. Waiting

34

for me to get home so he can call me and tell me what a good joke it was."

Alex would have something to tell Eddie, too. Wait until he told him he'd been picked up by the police. And questioned. Alex took more interest in the inside of the car now, trying to make out the switches for the lights and siren. He wondered where the rifles were. And the bulletproof vests. When they loaded his bike into the trunk, he was too excited to see what else was in there.

The back seat was molded plastic. Smooth hardness under his hands. No place to hide anything here. The odor was of a closed-in locker room. Wait till he told Eddie. And Candy. Would he build it up a little? Tell Eddie he had to lean against the side of the car while they patted him down? No. He didn't like to lie to Eddie.

A sudden hot awareness flooded his body. Heat radiated from the back pocket of his Levi's, from the small automatic that he'd stuck there. Good thing the police didn't shake him down. How could he explain the gun that belonged to Eddie's stepfather?

Think about something else. Don't think about the gun. He began to think about Eddie. Once more he saw Eddie dancing off through the golden leaves.

• • • Chapter Four

THE POLICE CAR turned in at the trailer park under the faded blue and orange sign that used to say BELVEDERE. Now the letters VEDERE were lighted by the one working bulb. The other letters were swallowed by murkiness. The car glided past the bank of eleven mailboxes at the curb. Dry, crooked-limb Chinese elms shielded the enclosure from street view, falsely suggesting gentility. The car sank into the deep rut just past the sidewalk, then ponderously rocked out the front wheels and eased in the rear ones.

All the windows were lighted in Eddie's home. Alex saw movement at the kitchen window as though someone were on the lookout for the police car. The kitchen door sprang open and the screen door erupted outward. Maria Rodriguez, Eddie's mother, bolted down the cinder-block steps.

The police car eased to a stop beside Boots's old green Maverick.

Alex sat trapped in his cage, the center of a maelstrom. Eddie's brothers and sister hugged the car. In the ugly glare of the arc lights, neighbors appeared on their stoops. The two policemen seemed to slow down. Every move was deliberate, as though they were onstage and had to make their audience see the meaning of every action they took. The officer named Pete took Alex's bicycle from the boxy trunk and put it carefully on the concrete pad. He leaned it against the stoop on which Boots stood.

Alex could see his mother, quiet, pale, waiting by the door. Her thin arms were folded across her chest, making her small against the cold of the autumn night. Her face was tight and anxious.

Deenie's face pushed against the car window, her wide eyes animal-like with their mascara. She turned to yell, "Hey, Mom. Eddie's not here." Pressed against the window again, she screeched, "Where's Eddie?"

Marlow opened the back door very carefully. With his body, he blocked out space for Alex to step into. Alex forgot his pack and stumbled over it. Marlow caught his arm, then after he was out, waited for him to pull the pack behind him.

A hand fastened onto Alex's arm like a talon. Maria Rodriguez thrust her face into his, like an awful mask carved by the light and shadows.

"Where is Eddie? Tell me, where is my son? For the love of God," she pleaded. Afraid, Alex stared into her open mouth. Metal glittered from a molar far in the back. He tried to pull away, then felt Marlow turn him and guide him toward his home.

The other officer bent over Mrs. Rodriguez and led

her away. With the crowd scattering in front of them, Alex felt Marlow pull him back toward the car. He watched, not quite understanding, as Marlow fumbled with the door handle. Then he realized that he was locking the patrol car.

Marlow motioned Boots, then Alex, into the trailer, then he went in himself. He closed the door in the face of Mando, Eddie's twelve-year-old brother. Alex felt bad about that, and about Eddie's mother. He felt responsible. Maybe if he'd done something different, Eddie would be here right now. But he couldn't think what he could have done.

. . .

If Eddie were here, things would be as they always were on Friday nights. They lived through the ordinariness of it. Eddie would be in the bedroom he shared with Mando and Bobby. They were stacked like cordwood in double bunks. The empty one above Eddie had been Johnny's. Its bare mattress would be covered with clean clothes, not yet folded. Sometimes during the week, the family just lived out of that pile, never getting them put away.

In his trailer, on an ordinary Friday night, Alex would be alone. Lying on his bed, he would leaf through the *Gander Mountain Catalog*. Looking at the ads for hiking boots, and binoculars in nonglare tree-bark camouflage, he would wonder what his grandparents would send him for Christmas. What could they afford this year? Their lives had changed as much as his since they moved to Arizona. They had the expense of moving, Alex knew, and the doctor's bills for Mom.

Then, on an ordinary night, he would sleep. Always there was an awareness, a waiting. Even in his sleep he somehow knew when Boots came in. He would sink deeper into sleep, as though he could relax his guard.

So, they waited out Friday nights. On Saturday and again on Sunday, he and Eddie rode to the mountains. Climbed until they came out into The Flats, with the broken-down shelter, the boulders, ponderosas, and firs. They came into the land they claimed as theirs, the territory of the Sandia Mtn. Trappers & Gold-Mining Co. Alex wished this were just an ordinary Friday night.

Marlow was very polite. He asked if he could sit at the kitchen table while he asked some questions. He looked from Alex to Boots as though searching for a family resemblance. There was one.

Both faces had broad, Slavic-looking cheeks, with high cheekbones. On the mother's face, the prominent ridge over the eyes rolled with lavender-shaded smoothness toward her brow. Thinly sketched lines made eyebrows that pointed off toward some spot high above her ears.

In Alex, the sandy eyebrows hugged the prominent ridge and with the high line of his cheekbones gave him a guarded look.

He took off his vest and then unbuttoned the top of his camouflage shirt. His neck was sticky from dried sweat. His mouth was dry and tasted of bad breath.

Boots smoothed her short, brown, fake-leather skirt over her thighs and sat down carefully. She was still in her barmaid clothes, even to the calf-high boots, red Justin Ropers. She smelled strongly of stale smoke and beer, always on her until she showered and washed her blond kinked hair. Alert, she looked at Marlow and Alex in turn, waiting. Her pale blue eyes looked flat, as though there was nothing behind them. A glass stood on the table in front of her, with diet Coke just covering the ice cubes. Alex moved it over to the kitchen counter and wiped the wet ring off the formica tabletop. He squeezed into the seat by the wall.

"Let's see. Let me get this down in the proper place. These forms. All this paperwork," Marlow said as though asking for their commiseration. Their eyes were as blank blue as glass marbles.

"Your name is Alex. Would that be Alexander? Yes? Alexander Grant. Fifteen years old. Student at Canyon High School. What grade, Alex? Freshman, huh? So, where did you go to school last year, son?"

Alex didn't like to be called son, especially by strangers, but he just looked down and didn't object.

"Las Cruces, huh? Did you just move here, then?"

"He did. I've lived here for about twelve years. Alex lived in Las Cruces with my parents until August," Boots answered. Her words came in short bursts. "My mother's got emphysema. My parents moved to Arizona to one of those retirement places where no kids are allowed."

To his next question, Boots answered, "My name's

Boots Ashley. That's my professional name. The one I go by."

Alex wished she hadn't said that. He wished she sounded, and looked, like a real mother. He wished she wouldn't keep slanting her eyes at Marlow that way.

"I'm really a dancer," she explained. "But I can't get work dancing. While I'm between jobs, I work at the Capital J Bar. I've been a cocktail waitress there for three years now." Alex knew Boots took pride in that. Most liquor-service people move around a lot. But he wondered why she didn't notice that three years made a long wait between dancing jobs.

"And your father, Alex?" the officer asked.

Alex glanced at Boots. She gave no sign of concern, looking curious, as if she, too, wondered what his answer might be.

"My parents are divorced," Alex said. "My father split when I was about three and I don't even know him."

"Tell me about Eddie Chavez," Marlow said.

"Well, when I moved up here in August, I met him. We hang out together. He's really about the only friend I have here. I mean, a friend I can do things with."

"So, you left here this morning? About what time?"

"We left here about quarter to eight to go to school. Before we got to the bus stop, we decided to ditch school and go to the mountains instead."

Alex heard Boots stir beside him. He kept his eyes down so he wouldn't have to look at her.

41

"You rode your bikes to the mouth of Embudito Canyon where you showed me?"

"Yep. Left them there. Then went up the canyon on foot."

"How far did you go? Can you give me an idea?"

"I can't say in miles. It's where the Transition Life Zone starts to change to the Canadian Life Zone."

Marlow looked up with a puzzled look on his face. Alex felt embarrassed. He hadn't been trying to show off some knowledge that Marlow didn't have. "Where the ponderosa trees peter out and the Douglas firs start. I don't remember what altitude that is, but it's not near the ridge. The canyon opens out into a flat place and there's an old lean-to there. It's on the topo map." Without even thinking, Alex had referred to the Geological Survey map the way his grandfather always did.

"Tell me about the last time you saw Eddie."

"He went off to hide and I was supposed to find him," Alex said. In his mind he did a fast replay of Eddie leaping into the air in the golden explosion. But he heard his own words come out as black and white while the scene playing in his head was in living color. When he watched Marlow's writing, he could see the officer squeeze down the black and white image. It became small and manageable and fit the lines on his report. Alex was dismayed by the way his memories were compressed into that cramped space.

"I waited till I couldn't hear him anymore, then I went to look," Alex continued. His mood changed as

42

he began to relive his frustration and fear. "I went to the lean-to first, where we hung out." Alex was careful not to say words like "play" which would mark him as a child. Nor was he going to mention their other activities on the mountain, activities that he knew would be labeled "fantasies." "Anyway, he wasn't anyplace around there."

"So, then what did you do?" Marlow asked.

"It was getting late and cold. I thought he might have gone ahead of me, and be waiting on the trail. You know, like an ambush." Alex looked at the tabletop. He knew adults thought you were lying if you didn't look them in the eye. But he was tired, too tired to come out of himself.

"He wasn't on the trail, and when I saw his bike was gone, I thought he went home. I already told you the rest. Remember? When you picked me up."

"Describe Eddie Chavez for me," Marlow said. The motor in the refrigerator clonked on, then settled into a high-pitched hum.

Alex picked at a cactus spine in his thumb. He must have gotten that when he was charging around looking for Eddie. "He's as tall as me. Not as heavy. Maybe 115 pounds. He has black hair and black eyes. Sometimes they're brown. I don't know. We wear the same size tennies. Reeboks." Eddie's beard was starting to come in, but Alex didn't see any reason to mention that. "When last seen, Eddie Chavez was wearing a black T-shirt that said 'Metallica' and black jeans." Alex jerked alert. He realized that he had mouthed the formula TV announcers use for missing persons.

Marlow looked up, too, as though to see if Alex was smarting off.

"Any scars, tattoos?"

"No. I don't remember any," Alex said. He didn't think the tattoo that Eddie tried to put on his hand would count. Eddie picked at his skin and inked it to make a caricature of a Chicano with a fedora, a Fu Manchu mustache, and sunglasses. Only the sunglasses took. So he had two black spots on the back of this hand.

"Did Eddie ever talk about running away?"

"No," Alex mumbled. Even this morning, with the bruise under his eye, Eddie had talked about leaving home. Alex didn't take him seriously. He was just letting off steam. He wouldn't leave the crowded trailer, the sound of his brothers' breathing in the night, the volatile Deenie, the baby being passed from hand to hand as the kids watched TV. Eddie's biggest sorrow for Johnny, in prison in Texas, was that he was so far away from his family.

"How did Eddie get along with his mother and father?" Marlow asked.

"I don't know," Alex said. To tell about Eddie and Paco Rodriguez would be to let Eddie down.

"You know, don't you, Alex, that if you and Eddie had gone to school today, we probably wouldn't have a problem now?" Marlow asked.

"Yes, sir." Alex couldn't argue with that.

"Have you been truant before, you and Eddie?"

Boots half rose and leaned forward with her hands

splayed on the table. "Officer, Alex is a good kid. No trouble. A's and B's in school. You can believe him. He's dependable. He doesn't cut classes. If it hadn't been for Eddie, he would have been in school today. Eddie . . . Well, you can't always tell what Eddie's going to do. He's scatterbrained. Like a little kid. No telling where he is."

"Yes, ma'am," Marlow said. He turned once more to Alex. "Tell me straight, Alex. Do you know where Eddie is?"

"No, I swear I don't. I think he's out on the mountain and needs help. But I don't know where he is."

Marlow pulled a card from a pocket in the back of the notebook and gave it to Alex. "If you think of anything else or if Eddie gets in touch with you, call that number," he said. To Boots he said, "Alex shouldn't go out again tonight. There is a curfew law, you know. Young people under eighteen are not allowed on the streets after eleven at night unless accompanied by a parent."

"No problem," she said. "He looks pretty beat anyway."

• • •

After Marlow left, after the patrol car pulled away, Boots took off her boots and stood in the middle of the kitchen in her stocking feet. Arms akimbo, she said plaintively, "Jeez, Alex, getting called home from work on a Friday night. One of my best nights. And getting mixed up with the police. The way it comes out on their records, it looks like you did something wrong. All because of Eddie. He's done some dumb thing and you're getting the heat."

"You mean he's done some dumb *Mexican* thing, Boots?"

"Well, yes. That is what I mean. You don't know. You haven't had the experience I have. Drunk Mexicans in the bar. You don't know how dumb they can be."

"Eddie's not a drunk Mexican in a bar. He doesn't even drink beer. Stop labeling people, Boots. It's not fair," Alex protested.

"It might not be fair, but it's true. They don't finish school. They won't speak English. I shouldn't have let you spend so much time with Eddie. Now, look. Police bringing you home in police cars. All because Eddie did something dumb."

"Yeah. He probably did a dumb Mexican thing like falling and getting hurt." All the tears in Alex welled up. Rather than direct any more of his frustration at Boots, he rushed into his bedroom and slammed the flimsy door. He curled into a knot and sobbed uncontrollably.

Outside his door he heard Boots saying, "Honey, I'm sorry. I like Eddie, too. It's gonna turn out OK."

When he finally cleared himself of most of his pent-up despair, he quietly went to the bathroom and showered. He went back to his room and set his alarm for five o'clock.

• • • Chapter Five

STANDING ON TIPTOE in the dry weeds outside the next-door trailer, Alex tapped on the little window. He knew this was the bedroom of Eddie's brothers. The sound of his fingernails was crystal clear. Again, in the cold morning darkness, he tapped. Finally Mando peeped from under the faded green curtain. By signs, Alex got him to open the window.

"Did Eddie come back last night?" Alex whispered.

"No. Mom made Deenie call everybody she could think of. All our family. Eddie's friends in the valley where we lived last year. She even called the pen in Texas where Johnny is, in case Eddie is going to see Johnny." Mando had dark circles around his eyes as though he hadn't slept much.

In five minutes, with his backpack strapped to his bicycle rack with elastic cords, Alex was on his way. He pumped his way through dark streets toward the darker bulk to the east that was the Sandia Mountains.

By the time the sky lightened, Alex had hidden his

bike under chamisa bushes at the big city water tank.

When he thought how easily he let Marlow make him believe that Eddie was OK, Alex felt heavy, his chest a solid mass. Last night Alex was almost convinced that the adults could handle things. "Well, they don't know anything," he thought, "because they won't listen. Eddie didn't run away. He's up there on that mountain — hurt. And his only chance of getting down is me."

He looked at the massive foothills that guarded the way into Embudito Canyon. Then on up, where he knew the blackness concealed stands of pines, firs, and spruces. Last night's snow lay like confectioner's sugar on the ridges. Inky clouds pressed down on the peaks, promising more snow.

"I hope it holds off," Alex thought. "Even in good weather, I might have a hard time finding Eddie if he's unconscious."

"I've got to think," he told himself. "I wish Pop was here." Alex groaned when he thought how he had acted yesterday. Like a little kid when it was getting late and he was hunting Eddie. Dashing here and there, sometimes going to the same place twice. Yesterday, he thought Eddie might have already gone down the mountain. Even so, he still couldn't excuse himself for being so dumb.

The need to hurry, to make up for yesterday, got to him. Panic exploded in his brain like popcorn. First one tiny pop, then more and more until his thinking powers were whited out.

"Hold up, son. Just get your head on straight." Alex

could almost hear his grandfather's deep, calm voice. "Backtrack over yesterday's trail. Cover every possibility. You can do it. You've got good stuff in you."

Alex went down the sandy arroyo to the rusted car body where he and Eddie had left their bikes yesterday. There was nothing that he hadn't seen last night when he was there with the police.

Then he went back up the arroyo past the dun-colored boulders that embraced the entrance to the canyon. Here, protected from last night's wind, all of yesterday's history was preserved in the loose sand. A record of the people from the city below who came here — hikers, birders, photographers, lovers, and Alex and Eddie. Their tracks were all here, but muddled, one on top of the other. There was no way to read the message.

So intent was Alex in looking for a sign, that he was startled when he caught movement from the corner of his eye.

The yellow eyes of a coyote locked with his. The coyote seemed unhurried but was in sight for only a fraction of a second before it melted into the hummocks of dry salt cedar. Alex marveled at how it was part of this place. The same color as the sand and bushes. Moving like a breeze. Yet it came out and showed itself when it wanted to. Maybe he would have powers like that when he was grown and living in the wilderness.

First there was only dry sand in the streambed, then splotches of moisture. Alex found the holes and mounds of sand left by the couple he saw yesterday when he came down. "Panning for gold," he thought. But they hadn't dug down far enough. They hadn't found any there.

As Alex worked his way up the canyon, he zig-zagged from one side to the other. Every clump of boulders, every stand of willows where Eddie might have lain in ambush, he checked out. By the time he had gone about thirty minutes up the trail, the stream was a continuous gurgle. The water braided itself like a clear rope across the smooth bottom. Leaves rotted with an acid woodsy smell. A thin layer of snow covered everything. Where the water ran slow and spread out, there was a layer of ice.

"I'm the first person up here today," Alex thought. "But I can't even find my own tracks from yesterday and I know I was here." Animals had come to the stream in the night. Those tracks he could recognize. Raccoon, deer. Of human trace he found none.

Close by, he came on bear tracks. Unmistakable, with the fine knife-edge lines made by the claws. Nearby was a pile of droppings, still steaming. "My gosh, I never thought about this," he said to himself. "I'll bet Eddie was scared last night. I'm scared right now." The air seemed to vibrate around him, and the soundtrack from *Grizzly Adams* pounded in his ears — the growling, tearing noises when the bear attacked. Fear ran through him like an electric shock. This was the first time he had been in the mountains alone.

"Maybe," he whispered, "I'll be the one who doesn't come back today. And there's no one who'll come looking for me. Only Boots knows I'm here. I can't picture Boots up here, looking. And the police will just think I've run away from home to join Eddie."

He waited until the sweat dried on his face, listened until all he heard was his own blood pulsing in his ears. But the bear sign spooked him. Through the underbrush, when he saw a spill of blood-red splotches, he stopped breathing. He knew, almost immediately, it was nothing human, knew it was red-leafed Virginia creeper. He moved slowly, scared now, turning often to check the trail behind him.

"Eddie," he called shyly, then more urgently. Calling and listening became partly a search pattern and partly noise to chase off the bear.

Alex found no trace of Eddie. Even when he finally came out to The Flats, there was no evidence that Eddie had been there yesterday.

Though the sky was overcast, the sun heated up the air enough to melt the thin layer of snow. Dampness lay on the fallen leaves and needles. Alex took off his quilted vest and hung it and his pack on the stub of a ponderosa limb. A sharp wind cut through his sweat-soaked back. When he sat down, the seat of his pants got wet from the leaves.

Alex forced himself to eat an orange and to drink water from his flask. "Don't be a fool, son," he could hear Pop saying. "You need your strength." The acid in the orange stung his chapped lips. His throat was sore and his head hurt from concentrating.

At the far side of The Flats, a Steller's jay hopped closer. It was nervous and tossed its black crest from side to side. Alex thought it looked like a small hang-man with a black hood from which white sinister eyes peered. He knew jays didn't have white eyes. "Spooky," he thought. "All the bird wants is food, yet I see evil signs in the way it looks."

The fruit gave him energy. Enough to concentrate on his mission again. "Damn that Eddie," he thought, "he ought to be here helping me." When he caught himself in this lapse of logic, he was shocked. Still he resented Eddie for deserting him.

"If Eddie had listened to me yesterday, he'd be here right now, hopping around and wanting to do this or that. What Boots said is true. Eddie is kind of crazy.

"But he's my friend. If no one else will search for him, I've got to." So Alex talked back and forth in his mind.

While he rested, the sky got darker. Big snowflakes, fat and wet, floated down and clung to every surface.

He jumped up and put his vest back on and shoved the pack into the old lean-to. The weather changed the picture. Now he had to hurry before the snow covered everything. He stood in the shelter for a min-ute to make a plan. Rushing around the way he did yesterday was no good.

"I've got to think like Eddie. I know he didn't leave the canyon yesterday. I'm pretty sure he didn't sneak down the canyon and try to ambush me. That means he hid someplace around here. It wasn't very long after he left that I started to look for him. How long? Five minutes? I was drowsy. Did I sleep?"

So, Eddie was in sight. Then, out of sight. Then,

shortly after that, he was out of hearing distance. If he had heard Alex coming toward him, he might have sneaked farther away. If he were on an outcrop he could have moved without making noise.

Alex checked the boulders first. He peered into the crannies and nooks where boulders fell together and created caves and tunnels under them. Eddie could have fallen into one of these holes. He was surely hurt if he ended up here. All the time Alex looked, the snow kept smothering him, coming down, coming sideways, clinging to his face and eyelids. "Eddie, Eddie," he called. His voice served to keep him company as well as to reach out for Eddie.

By the stream, under the umbrella folds of the big fir tree, he stopped to get some shelter from the onslaught of the snow. He looked at the sign and remembered how he and Eddie had gouged out the letters with a knife and an old chisel:

SANDIA MTN. TRAPPERS
& GOLD-MINING CO.

They filled the grooves with Wite-Out that Eddie had lifted from the desk of the typing teacher.

The result was so audacious that for two weekends they didn't dare put it in plain sight. For them, that action was as bold as Columbus claiming a new world. They finally agreed to nail it to the trunk of this fir whose sweeping branches hid it from view.

The sign reminded Alex that there had been mining on this mountain in the old days. There could be mine shafts, overgrown, treacherous. There was nothing he could do about them, except try to keep out of them.

He shook himself like a dog, and went to the stream bank to check for prints. There were the delicately divided heart imprints made by deer hoofs last night. The prints he and Eddie made yesterday had a fine crust of ice and were easily identifiable. If Eddie had run along here in his search for a hiding place, his feet would have dug up sand and pebbles. There was no sign of running feet.

Up the bank from the stream, he moved across white snow, through white snow, with a white snow netting hanging from his hair and eyebrows. He followed the old trail that ran on up to the South Crest. Slipping, he went down on his hands and knees among the sharp rocks. Even though blood seeped from his scraped palm, the cold numbed the pain.

He stopped to check out the copse of scrub oak where he and Eddie had done their only trapping. Drops of his own red blood on the snow brought back the memory.

Late on a Saturday afternoon in September, they had set out a trap big enough for a wood rat. Alex had read about traps and thought he knew which Conibear trap would be the best one for their purposes. But the only kind readily available was the big rat trap from the supermarket. After wiring it to a sapling, they baited it with Velveeta cheese.

Sunday morning they rushed up the canyon to check the trap. The metal bar had snapped shut on the neck and paw of a ground squirrel. It was still alive. The paw kept the bar from crushing the neck of the animal. There were signs that it had flailed around, trying to jerk itself free of the trap. Its orange-shaded body shivered as Alex and Eddie bent over it. White rings circling the eyes made them look more scared. The open mouth showed yellow teeth and a yellower bit of cheese held there. Blood dribbled from the grimace. Even as bedraggled as its fur was from the struggle, its grayish white belly and the black stripe down its back excited Alex. He ran a finger down the stripe, feeling the warmth and pounding fear.

Eddie, excited, too, started to open the trap. "What'll we do with it?" he asked. "It's too little to skin."

"Wait," Alex said. "If you open the trap it might run away. It's injured and you're not supposed to let injured animals get away."

"I don't want to let it loose," Eddie said. "I want to do something with it. Hey, man, did you ever hear of a chipmunk fur coat? Maybe for a Barbie doll." Eddie breathed out his funny laugh and his mouth stayed open ready to laugh again.

"It's no good to us. We'll have to kill it."

Without hesitation, Eddie put the creature, still in the trap, on a rock and hit it on the head with another rock. Instead of cracking open like a walnut, the skull burst. Bits of tissue and blood spattered them both. Eddie held up his arm, the inside of his wrist splashed with gore.

"Man, look at that. It looks like I killed something big with my bare hands. Maybe I'll leave this on to show Mando and Bobby."

"Aw, Eddie, go wash it off. It's not that big a deal."

55

Alex felt sick. It was the way he always felt when he saw films of the Jack Kennedy assassination and the pieces of skull and brain flying over the back of the open car and Jackie Kennedy trying to reach them.

Now, thinking of the cheese in the teeth, the cheese the ground squirrel didn't even get to swallow, Alex unconsciously twisted his neck trying to free himself from some trap.

And Eddie. "Is Eddie dead? Has he been dead since yesterday, his head cracked open on some rock? If he is alive, he won't be after today," Alex thought grimly. "This storm will finish him off.

"I'll be finished, too, if I don't get off this mountain. I have to give up. I can't find him. I've got to get myself out of here before this wind starts to freeze me."

The damp snow made his footing slippery as he worked his way down the canyon. Anxiety diluted his concentration. Several times, he skidded and fell down the slopes. A twist the wrong way could leave him crippled and helpless.

• • • Chapter Six

ALEX AWOKE SUNDAY morning shivering in his narrow bed. Through sticky eyelashes, he saw that it was six minutes past eight. His throat was raw and his nose dripped like an icicle in the sun. He stumbled into the bathroom to search for a box of tissues. A solid headache sat right behind his eyes.

Opening the medicine cabinet, he pawed through tubes of cosmetics, vials of diet pills, and vitamins. What did his grandmother give him for a cold? Aspirin and orange juice. He held the aspirin in his mouth until it melted and ran down his throat. It tasted awful. The orange juice tasted as though it had been poured over rusty nails.

Outside the sky was dark. A low rumpled cloud cover hung over the Heights. No one was stirring at the Chavez/Rodriguez trailer. So far as Alex could tell from looking out the window, Eddie's bike was not in its hiding place at the back of the trailer.

With a magnet, Boots had stuck a note on the refrigerator door. Written in bold red strokes, it read, "Alex. Stay here. Do not leave. I MEAN IT."

Alex didn't feel like going anywhere except back to bed. He put another blanket on his bed, then threw it off when he began to sweat.

From the top of his chest of drawers, he took a book on backpacking and thumbed it open to the chapter called "Danger!" It said just what he remembered it saying: "Hypothermia is a big killer of beginning hikers. A condition where the body loses more heat than it generates, hypothermia is often brought on by wind chill, and aggravated by moisture."

Alex remembered last night. The TV weatherwoman had predicted that the temperature would be in the low thirties at the Crest on the Sandia Mountains. The book gave a table showing that if the wind speed was only 10 mph and the measured temperature was 30 degrees, the wind-chill temperature would be 16 degrees.

"And Eddie only wearing a short-sleeved shirt," Alex thought. "He's frozen for sure, even if he fell into a mine shaft and is out of the wind. I should have made him put on his jacket."

Before Alex thought out how he could have made Eddie put on a jacket, he was asleep.

A dream came, full and real. He was back in Cruces, living with Mom and Pop. Mom was still healthy and was coddling him because he was sick. "Here, sweetie. Take this honey and vinegar. It'll make that nasty sore throat feel better." Alex could hear Pop, too, though he couldn't quite see him. "Don't baby him so, Maggie. As soon as you get better, Alex, we'll go look for Eddie. I'll help you. I know where to look." The dream popped open in Alex's head.

He realized the phone was ringing in the living room. Grabbing a fistful of tissues to sop up his nose, he rushed to answer it.

Out of the dream, and on the other end of the telephone line, Alex heard his grandfather. "Hold on, Pop," he said. He covered the receiver and yelled, "Boots, it's Pop on the phone." Into the phone, he said, "Pop, I've got to talk with you. I've got to —"

"Just a minute, son. Hold on. Let me say my piece first. Is your mother there? I want to tell you both at once."

Boots came down the hall, her eyes still puffy from sleep. She took the phone and held it so that both she and Alex could hear. Her snaky hair tickled the side of Alex's face.

"Boots, Alex," Pop began. "Margaret is in the hospital. Just a little touch of pneumonia. But it could be very serious because of her emphysema. It's a good thing we moved to this place. The doctor here was on top of things right away."

"How long do you think she'll be in the hospital, Pop?" Boots asked.

"We don't know yet. But if you try to call me and I'm not home, it's because I'm at the hospital with your mother. I spend all my time there. They even bring me a lunch."

"Don't you get sick, Pop," Boots said.

"Yeah, and Pop, tell Mom we're thinking of her,"

Alex added. He didn't try to say anything about Eddie. After the phone call, Boots said, "You're rotten with a cold. I suppose you spent all day yesterday on the mountain. Up there with the snow and snakes."

Even in his misery, Alex smiled at Boots's ideas about the mountains. He had grown up thinking of her more as a big sister than a mother. He'd always called her Boots.

On her infrequent visits to Cruces, they did exciting things like going to the Sonic Drive-in where the high school kids hung out. Or sometimes she took him to the park where he practiced with his skateboard on concrete ramps.

"I was looking for Eddie," he told her. "I couldn't find him. I wanted to ask Pop what I should do."

"He's got enough to think about without worrying him with that, Alex."

From the table, she picked up the card the policeman had left. "I wonder if he's married," she said.

"Who?" Alex spoke in a voice muffled by tissues.

"Marlow. R. Marlow," Boots replied. She stretched out on the narrow strip of floor between the couch and the TV, and began to scissor her legs. Alex didn't pay any attention. This was something she did every day so she'd be ready when she got a dancing job.

At the sound of a car, Alex looked out the window. A four-wheel-drive vehicle stopped outside Eddie's trailer. A man wearing an institutional gray uniform stood on the stoop and knocked. Alex couldn't see the shoulder patch.

60

"There's some cop or something at Eddie's trailer," Alex told Boots.

"He'll probably be here next. I'll put on some clothes," she said.

Alex already had sweats on. He watched until the man came out of the next-door trailer, mounted their stoop, and knocked at the door. By the time Alex let him in and he was introducing himself, Boots was back in the room. Alex had never known her to get dressed so fast.

"I'm Dan Baylor. We're going to do a search for Eddie Chavez in the mountains. I'm with the Search and Rescue Team." He was very polite and didn't sit down on the worn couch until Boots asked him to.

"I went up yesterday. I couldn't find him," Alex blurted.

"Did you go alone?" Mr. Baylor asked.

"Yeah. Eddie's the only friend I got who goes to the mountain with me."

"You shouldn't go alone. People see the mountains from the city, and they look familiar to them. They think there's no danger to them. But I've carried the injured off there. I can't tell you the times. And searched for the lost. Not just little kids either."

Alex already knew this, knew he shouldn't go alone. He remained silent. Even through the brain numbness caused by his cold, he began to feel some hope. Someone finally believed him. He suspected Eddie's mother had prodded and prodded to get some action. Maybe they would find Eddie. Maybe it wasn't too late.

Mr. Baylor still scolded. He was delivering his message to Boots now. "Keep him home, Ma'am. Don't let him go up there by himself. We don't want to be looking for two missing boys." Boots shook her head vigorously, looking quite maternal.

He drew maps out of a plastic case. "Can I put these on the table?" He spread out a Geological Survey map with Embudito Canyon in big scale. Contour lines showed the rises in elevation — squeezed close together for a cliff or escarpment, wide apart for a gentle slope. "Alex, can you show me where you and Eddie went on Friday?"

Alex had a map like this one, except on a smaller scale. When he and Eddie had first started going up in the mountains, he had marked all the landmarks on his map. He put his fingers where the big city water tank stood and jumped to the mouth of the canyon. Then he traced the stream's little blue thread into the mountain. He stopped at a triangular symbol that looked something like a tent.

"Right here. This is sort of our headquarters. This shelter is falling down now. See, the Forest Service trail doesn't go by it now. That trail's over on this slope."

Alex was silent for a moment. Then, with his finger he traced a spiral starting at the shelter and winding away from The Flats. "I looked all around here yesterday. Everyplace we ever went. Then the snow came. I couldn't see. I had to give up and come home," he said.

"What was Eddie wearing? Shoes. What kind?

Hat?" Mr. Baylor made notes in a neat notebook. When Alex said that Eddie had no cap or hat and was not wearing a jacket, Mr. Baylor shook his head. "When will people learn?"

"I hope you find him, and he's . . . I hope you find him," Alex said.

"So do I, son."

. . .

After the man left, Alex reminded Boots that he hadn't bought any groceries yesterday. "Get more orange juice, OK?" he asked her.

"I haven't had enough sleep. But I'm wide-awake. Might as well go to the store now and conk out later." Boots's blond hair bounced like springs and she looked perky, despite pouchy half-moons under her eyes. Boots always complained about not getting enough sleep. Because she worked late hours at the bar, she was deep in sleep when the world around her burst awake before dawn and began its noisy daytime activities.

. . .

Alex turned on the TV and turned it off. He picked up the book he was reading for Language Arts, and found himself staring right through the pages. He telephoned Candy.

"Hey, there, Alex. What happened to you and Eddie Friday?"

Candy's voice filtered through his ringing ears and he wondered why he hadn't thought to call Candy before this. "We cut school and went up in the mountains. Eddie didn't come back. He's lost or something."

Alex told Candy the whole story, about the police and the Search and Rescue Team. He had to explain some details because Candy had never been — would never be — in a canyon, climbing over boulders or panning for gold.

Candy punctuated his tale with little whistles, clucks, and "wow's."

"I feel like it's my fault," Alex said. "Like I should have made Eddie come to school on Friday. Or made him come off the mountain when it was time. Or made him wear a jacket."

"You can't make Eddie do anything he doesn't want to do," Candy said. "He's stubborn — as stubborn as a mule. You coming to school tomorrow?" Candy asked.

"Yeah, I guess so. I got a bad cold, but since I missed Friday, I'd better go."

"They'll find Eddie," Candy said. "They'll have him in some hospital this evening being hand-fed. I see it on TV all the time."

• • •

Alex was wrapped in a blanket and dozing on the couch when Boots came back.

"My gosh. The most awful thing happened," she said. She flung the two bags of groceries on the counter. Her face was a misery. "I hit this cat. I was going slow, but it ran right in front of me. An orange and white one. I couldn't stop. I felt it hit." She turned her face away and said, "I found a place to park. I was almost sick. But I went back to see if it was still alive. Just injured. You know. To take it to a vet, if it was still alive. But it wasn't there. I looked. I even went into people's yards. But I couldn't find it."

"Maybe it wasn't really hurt, Boots. Just bumped a little," Alex said. His voice sounded far away, separated from his ears by a thick barrier.

"No. It's someplace, hurt and suffering. I know it is and it's my fault."

At these words, Alex had a brief recall of ground squirrel brains and blood splashed everywhere. "Like Eddie," Alex said.

"What? What're you saying?" Boots's words burst out. "Eddie's OK. They'll find him. And if he's hurt, it's his own fault. It's not your fault."

The memory of the spattered ground squirrel persisted. He didn't understand Boots. How could she section off her feelings? Be almost hysterical about the cat but not care about Eddie? He didn't feel well enough to think about it. "If I'm asleep, wake me before you go to work, huh? I'm supposed to watch that TV show tonight at seven. The one about the day after a nuclear attack on the United States."

Boots made a face. "What's the good of something like that? Making high school kids worry about something none of us can do anything about."

• • •

Before she left, Boots woke Alex. She had fixed him some soup — tomato. No chicken soup for her. She didn't like chicken and couldn't imagine that anyone else might. The table was cleared and the groceries put away. Alex sensed an effort to be orderly. Order didn't usually follow Boots's activities.

He went into the bathroom, still steamy from her shower. He felt as though he shouldn't be there. This room with its undercurrent of her skin and hair odor should be visited by someone who was not her son. Her underpants and exercise bra were on the floor and the curling iron was still plugged in. He picked up her underclothes to put them in the hamper. The thin nylon clung to his rough hands. A feeling he thought of as a *zizzle* spiraled through him. He shook his hand impatiently to rid it of the fabric. Not for the first time did he wish Boots were more like a mother.

He heard her call from the living room, where she was ready to leave. "Eddie's family will probably be on TV tonight. I saw the TV van over there. And the police. I went outside and asked. They didn't find him."

When she saw Alex's face, she took her hand from the doorknob and came over to him. She put both arms around him and tried to pull his head onto her shoulder as if he were a little boy. She even patted him on the back. "I'm sorry, Alex. I really am." She pulled away and looked at him. "Well, it probably means he wasn't up there. He probably came down before you did and ran away. Just like the police thought on Friday night."

Her face lighted up. "It's probably better. See, if

he's with friends or something, he's much safer. Not like being in the mountains with all the snow and the snakes."

She continued. "The TV people, they wanted to talk with you, too. I just said you were sick. I don't think the police can give out your name because you're a minor. Eddie's family must have told them. Now, you stay here. I don't want you going out. And I don't want you opening the door to anyone."

Alex didn't feel like arguing. His nose dripped and his head was filled with a steady roar.

While Boots watched, Alex spooned up some soup. As soon as she left, he put the spoon down. He couldn't eat anything.

Later, he snapped on the TV. The news was just coming on. Something about the anniversary of Kennedy's assassination. University Lobo Football Team something, something.

"Two fifteen-year-old boys cut school on Friday. One of them, Canyon High student Eddie Chavez, has disappeared. His parents last saw him when he left to go to school Friday morning." Alex waited, but didn't hear his own name.

A quick shot showed the entrance to Belvedere Court. Then, Eddie's mother with Bobby and Deenie. All outside, standing beside their trailer. Eddie's mother didn't have a coat on and she looked small and cold. Rigidly, in front of her chest, she held a picture of Eddie so the camera could focus on it.

She look tired, so worn and tired. "If you saw Eddie Chavez on Friday or later, please call the police. If

anybody knows anything about my boy, please tell."
As she talked, she looked right out of the TV screen
at Alex. He closed his eyes. When he opened them,
he saw Eddie's picture. "Probably his school picture
from last year," Alex thought. He looked rounder,
more self-conscious, than Alex remembered him.

The announcer's voice took on a somber note.
"Search and rescue teams combed the Embudito Canyon of the Sandias today for the missing boy. The
search was hampered by the heavy snow that fell Saturday. It failed to turn up any trace of the missing
boy. According to a police spokesman, young Chavez
was with another fifteen-year-old Canyon High student. The companion said the two boys spent the day
in Embudito Canyon, and Eddie disappeared there.
His companion returned alone.

"When asked why the police had not begun the
search earlier, the spokesman said there was reason
to believe Chavez might have run away from home
instead of being lost on the mountain. Police have not
ruled out the possibility of foul play," the announcer
added.

The phone rang. It was Candy. "What do they
mean — foul play?" he asked.

"They haven't believed anything I've said," Alex
replied. He felt numb. He forced himself to say, "They
wouldn't look for him when I told them he was up
there. They thought I was lying. They thought he ran
away. Now they think he might be on the mountain
and dead. So, they want to blame me for killing him."

• • • Chapter Seven

Alex Grant sat in Mr. Plemmy's office awaiting the school counselor. As soon as he entered his first period class this Monday morning, the teacher handed him a note directing him to come here.

He had never been here before, did not know that this warren of little offices existed. The desk was piled high with papers. On top of the mess were two student-record folders. By laboriously spelling out the names upside-down, Alex saw that they were his and Eddie's.

The metal folding chair creaked as Alex examined the bulletin board by the door. There was a large calendar for November with events scribbled into the white boxes. Next to it was a cartoonlike poster. A small, miserable-looking boy in medieval clothes, his hands tied behind him with a heavy rope, was labeled "Freshman." He was standing in front of a desk labeled "Counselor." Leaning across the desk, threatening the freshman, was a large figure, its head covered with a hangman's black hood. For just a fraction of a second, the image of the Steller's jay with its evil look — the jay he had seen in the mountains on Saturday — flashed in Alex's mind. He turned away from the picture. It was probably meant to be funny.

His camouflage shirt was buttoned up to his neck. Despite the fact that his cuffs rode uncomfortably high on his wrists, they, too, were buttoned. Nervous, he folded and refolded his hall pass from first period.

Just as Alex had a tissue out and was ready to blow his nose, a middle-aged man whipped through the door. A small paunch stretched his Western-style shirt tight above his big brass belt buckle. His square shoulders pushed high as though to defend against some blow. Cowboy-boot heels thudded against the vinyl tiled floor.

Threading quickly around Alex's chair and a table, he got himself seated at his desk. He tilted his chair back with his hands clasped behind his head and beamed at Alex. There was an expectant silence.

"Well, laddie, what can I do for you?" he asked.

Alex showed the pass and said, "You sent for me."

His chair crashed forward and he picked up the top folder. "Oh, yes. You're Eddie Chavez."

Alex stiffened and became very alert. Surely this man knew about Eddie's disappearance. It was on TV last night. Probably in the newspaper this morning. And motor-mouth Stella, who rode the bus with Alex, would have spread it through the school by now.

Then apparently Mr. Plemmy saw Eddie's school

picture in the folder. He put it down and picked up the other one.

Alex could see the few pages in his folder. It was like the report the policeman Marlow had written down. Eight years of school life — of reading and tetherball, Miss Armstead and Mr. Lucero, Pablo and Neal, cafeteria and artwork in the halls — all squeezed down into those little spaces. All reduced from living color to little lines. As though it somehow wasn't very significant.

"No. Alexander Grant. Is that right? Well, Alexander, we seem to have a problem here. You and Eddie missed all your classes on Friday. Do you have a note from your parents saying you were sick or something? No? Were you truant, then?" Mr. Plemmy was registering seriousness, but Alex was watching his mouth. He was a juicy talker and seemed to have some trouble keeping his saliva under control.

"Yes, sir," Alex said.

"I notice you have a good attendance record since you came here. From Las Cruces, huh? Yes. Good record there, too." He stopped talking to wipe his hand across his mouth.

"Now, Alexander, you might not think one day is so bad. But it's a beginning, you see, one that could get you started on the wrong foot in high school." He leaned back in his chair again and continued. "You young lads come to high school and it's a whole new ball game . . ." He settled into what was evidently an often-repeated speech. Alex gazed past him out the narrow window. Above the ranks of houses and leaf-less treetops, he could just make out the ridge line of the Sandias. Purple, impassive. With Eddie Chavez enfolded into their surface, becoming part of them.

"... Eddie Chavez." When he heard Eddie's name coming from Mr. Plemmy's mouth, Alex again switched to alert. It didn't sound like a question. To cover up his inattention, Alex started a cough way down in his lungs, rattled it up his throat, and nearly sprayed it across the desk before he throttled it with a tissue.

Mr. Plemmy looked alarmed but continued. "Where is Eddie today?" he asked. Alex didn't believe the innocence in his bland face.

"I don't know."

"But you were together on Friday, weren't you?"

"Yes, sir," Alex said.

"Did you see Eddie on Saturday or Sunday?" Mr. Plemmy slid the question out as though it was the most natural thing in the world to inquire about Alex's activities on weekends.

Alex said, "Harumph," and began another cough.

"Do you know of any reason that Eddie might want to run away from home?" Mr. Plemmy dropped any pretense of innocence. He knew Eddie was missing.

Alex didn't answer, just creaked his weight around on the folding chair. He didn't look at the counselor but kept his eyes resolutely fixed on the mountains.

"Well, if there's any question of child abuse, or anything like that in Eddie's home, we need to know about it. We're trained to handle that kind of thing."

Mr. Plemmy must have sounded prissy even to his own ears. He banged his chair down. His hands went to his throat and tightened the silver bolo tie.

His voice deepened as he said, "I see you're from a single-parent home. Now, son, there are often problems when children live with just the mother. Lack of supervision, discipline, and so on." The counselor's voice in its deeper register droned on in another set lecture.

Alex resented this kind of talk, especially from a stranger. As he did a slow burn, he thought, "So, Boots and I have problems. But she's trying to support both of us. Why doesn't this joker pick on someone else? My father, for example. The missing Henry Grant, who never sends money, never shows any interest in his son."

"And then, there's the matter of culture, too," Mr. Plemmy said, leaning across the desk as though sharing a secret.

"What is he talking about?" Alex wondered to himself.

"Conflicts are bound to arise. Natural enough. They're different from us. A family like Eddie's. They've got different values. Why, if you two lads had a little conflict — things got out of hand, say. If one of you got hurt, let's say, why, people would understand."

Even though Alex understood now, he could scarcely believe what he was hearing. Mr. Plemmy represented the school and the teachers who taught about how great it was that New Mexico had three cultures. Anglo, Spanish, and Indian. But this man was inviting him to confess that he had fought with Eddie, maybe hurt him. And people would understand because Eddie was Mexican.

"Did you and Eddie have a fight?" he asked straight out, as though getting tired of trying to gain Alex's confidence.

Alex sat mute. He would not answer this man.

"Don't get sullen, now, lad. You're going to need to talk with someone. You're going to need someone like me in your corner. Just remember — " A knock on the door interrupted this warning.

A student aide handed Mr. Plemmy a note. He glanced at it, then said, "There's a juvenile officer here to speak with you, lad." He wiped his hand across his mouth and stood up. Scooping the folders off his desk, he led Alex down the hall to another small office.

In this room, there was a gray metal table and two chairs, one on either side of the table. There was no window, no bulletin board. The fluorescent tubes crackled overhead.

A young woman, short but erect, rose from one of the chairs. From behind big-framed glasses, brown eyes locked onto Alex's and held him. She thrust her hand forward. He was surprised. He had never seen anyone shake hands with a student in school. "Alexander Grant?" she said. "I'm Lily Torres." Her handshake was firm and brief.

She took the folders from Mr. Plemmy and thanked him. He seemed inclined to stay. She stood, holding the doorknob until he left. As she closed the door, he still stood in the hall. Alex sat down in the nearest chair. From a briefcase she withdrew a folder and a tablet of yellow lined paper.

"First, let me look at your file. Not bad. You've got mostly B's and C's. A good record." She looked up. "Are you interested in sports?"

"Yeah, sure. But in school, there are too many kids in PE to have good games. In Cruces, I used to play basketball with my friends in the park. That's more fun."

"You don't go out for varsity sports?"

"Naw. I'm not good enough. There are really good players in a school this big. Besides, I'd rather spend my time backpacking or camping."

"Do you belong to any clubs? After-school clubs?"

"Naw. I have to ride the bus. So I can't stay."

"Well, you probably know I'm here about Eddie's disappearance. May I call you Alex? Alex, I want you to go over again with me everything you told Officer Marlow." She dropped her gaze while she rummaged in the briefcase for a pen.

Alex took a deep breath. In a voice that cracked halfway through, he said, "I'm supposed to have a lawyer. Right? I'm supposed to be read my rights. Right?"

"No, Alex. You've not been charged with any crime. We're just trying to find out where Eddie is. If you tell the truth then there's nothing to worry about." She smiled directly at Alex. Her gentleness made it very difficult to deny her what she wanted.

"I've been telling the truth. Everything I said was

the truth. If the police had believed me, they would have searched for Eddie on Friday or Saturday. Maybe found him." Alex kept on, saying more than he intended to. "And on TV news last night, they said, 'Foul play.' Like I did something to hurt Eddie."

Alex got caught up in detailing the bad deal he felt he was getting. "And him," he said, jerking his thumb toward the door where Mr. Plemmy had stood, "practically accused me of killing Eddie."

Her head jerked up and her mouth tightened a little. "Who do you mean?"

"Him, Plemmy."

"What exactly did he say?"

"He was talking about cultures not mixing. He said if there was conflict and someone got hurt, he said he could understand that." What a level look she had, Alex thought. She has a Spanish name. She must have some feelings about what Plemmy said, but she still kept that little smile on her face.

"Could you just tell me again, Alex, about Friday? You were probably tired when you talked to Officer Marlow. You may have left out something important. Or maybe you've remembered something that might help us." Ms. Torres spoke in a matter-of-fact way.

"I told him everything. I told him Eddie was on the mountain. He didn't believe me. I told the Search and Rescue guy where Eddie was. It was probably too late then."

"You mean, you think Eddie is dead?" Ms. Torres asked.

"Yes, ma'am." Tears welled up in Alex's eyes and he made a big thing out of blowing his nose and getting his throat cleared. "Bad cold," he said. "Bad cold since Saturday night."

"Alex, were there any vehicles parked at the trailhead when you and Eddie went through the gate to get to the trail?"

He jerked his head up. What was she thinking? "There might have been a car or truck parked there. But there are houses all around. Some of those people might park there," he said.

"Think carefully, now. Who did you see Friday? After you left the bus stop?"

"No one we knew. We sneaked back to the trailer court to get our bikes and stuff."

He thought for a second. "People go in the canyon mostly on weekends, I guess. Wait. Someone was panning for gold in the canyon. On Saturday when I went up, I saw where they had been digging. I think I saw them when I came down Friday, but I don't think they were there when Eddie and I went up."

Lily Torres wrote a sprawling record on the tablet. Maybe she could put it down the way it really was. Alex caught himself thinking of Eddie's laugh and his disappearance into the golden explosion of leaves. Maybe she'd understand how it was. Maybe she'd know how to find Eddie and bring him back.

Off in the distance, the bell rang to end the first period. There was a rush of footsteps, a scrambling like that of a great herd of animals stampeding.

Ms. Torres cocked an ear toward the bell and smiled, as though she had memories of being part of that herd.

"What can you tell me about Eddie's family?"

"Nothing," Alex said. She ought to know better than to ask that. She wouldn't answer questions about her friend's family. Alex had been friends with enough kids from Hispanic homes to know they kept a strict silence against outsiders.

"I mean, was Eddie happy at home?" she asked.

"I don't know," Alex said.

"Did he talk about running away?"

"I don't remember."

A look of annoyance crossed her face. "Alex, we need all the information we can get if we're going to find Eddie. Maybe he's up on the mountain as you think. But maybe you're wrong. Maybe he ran away from home. There are many runaways out there in the streets. They do desperate things just to stay alive."

She shoved the yellow pad and the manila folder into her briefcase. Leaning forward, she locked Alex into the power of her steady brown eyes. "I used to be a high school counselor — down in the valley. I know Johnny Chavez, Eddie's brother. I sat in a room like this and talked with him and his mother. How do you think Eddie's mother will feel if Eddie goes the way Johnny did?"

Eddie wouldn't do that, Alex felt sure. Eddie wouldn't even drink a beer or try a cigarette, he was so afraid of ending up like Johnny.

• • • Chapter Eight

THIRD PERIOD. Career Exploration. Miss Jernigan. It was a big class. All thirty seats in the room
were assigned, but there were always absentees. The
misery of Alex's cold pressed down on him. The im-
plication of his two interviews weighed him down
even more.

He knew, before the last bell rang, that students
who had never looked at him before knew who he
was now. They looked at Eddie's empty desk. Until
today, he and Eddie had been anonymous. Almost
invisible except to each other, and Candy. Alex could
not trust himself to look at the empty desk. He pulled
himself inside the boundary of the camouflage shirt
and stared at his desk.

The bell rang. Little sounds of inattention caused
Alex to look up. He was not the center of interest
anymore. There was a new student. A girl stood by
Miss Jernigan's desk holding out a slip of paper. She
was the Gwen Martens, hat and all, from English class,

who occupied such a large place in Alex's thoughts. Miss Jernigan initialed the paper. Both she and the newcomer looked about the classroom for an available seat. Finally, Alex heard Miss Jernigan say, "Well, just for now."

Gwen came to the desk beside Alex's, the one that was assigned to Eddie. She put most of her books on the rack under the desk. Turning to Alex, she may have given him a tentative smile. A smile that acknowledged that he was a familiar face from English class. Alex didn't know what she did. As soon as he saw her sit in Eddie's place, he resumed studying the heart gouged into his desk top. The message, filled with dirt from an endless stream of semesters, said: CON AMOR CONCHA Y RUBEN.

Miss Jernigan stood behind her desk checking her roll book. The door to the corridor was open. The familiar *thunk-swoosh* noise made cavernous echoes in the now-empty hall as its steady rhythm advanced. As it came closer to the door, she snapped the book closed and waited.

Candelario Arellano swung his short crutches forward in the *thunk*, then pulled his body through the arc on the *swoosh*.

Because of the danger to him of being in crowds, he was allowed to arrive late to his classes. "Good morning, Miss." He spoke to Miss Jernigan with such a flourish that you expected to see him bow and tip a hat. Everything Candy did was a production. He was the center of attention, the star, wherever he was.

For him, with his short fragile bones and the body

80

of a ventriloquist's dummy, walking was a production. Coming down the crowded aisle between the desks, and swinging his briefcase onto the desk, then hoisting himself into the chair, was as riveting as any tail-swishing cheerleader in drill uniform. Also, Candy had a purpose about him. He was there to entertain. He was like a game-show host; the show didn't start until he was there to start it. He smiled genially all around, and may even have sent some silent signal to Miss Jernigan to start the class.

The buzzes, the glances directed at Eddie's desk continued. "Let's quiet down, please," the teacher began.

She wore flat heels and planted herself firmly in front of the class. Someone near the back caught her attention and she shook her head. "Not now, Buddy Jack. No interference, please. Let me explain your assignment first, then you can ask questions."

Buddy Jack asked his question anyway. "Miss. Isn't Eddie Chavez, the one who's missing — isn't that his desk?" Buddy Jack's voice had already changed and it rumbled from his oversize body.

"Yes, stupid. I told you that," Alex heard Audrey's voice say. He stared straight into the carved heart on his desk.

Miss Jernigan ignored the question and started explaining something about a questionnaire. Her voice was a drone in Alex's ears and his mind drifted back to Ms. Torres.

Chairs scraped and bumped around him, and Alex looked up, surprised. "Turn your desk this way,

Sport," he heard Candy saying from behind him. Without getting up, he dragged his desk around and made the top touch Candy's.

"What are we supposed to do?" Alex asked.

"Fill in this questionnaire about what we're going to do when we're grown-up." Candy lowered his voice and whispered, "Why weren't you on TV last night?"

"My mom says they can't identify me because I'm underage."

"Boy, I'd like to be on. I'd dazzle them." Alex didn't understand what Candy meant by that. Sometimes he could be a little weird.

Miss Jernigan stopped by their desks. "I'm going to put someone else with you since your group's so small." If she knew why Eddie wasn't there, she gave no sign of it. She turned and motioned to Gwen, who got up and slowly moved her desk to touch theirs. "Gwen, meet your classmates, Alex and Candy," Miss Jernigan said and left them.

Alex felt the heat rising in his face. He'd have to talk with her. Even look straight at her instead of watching her secretly. Today she had on a white felt hat, like one you might see in an old movie. Not a fedora like the Mexican girls wore sometimes — a woman's hat. A long, full skirt just touched the tops of lace-up boots. She looked old-fashioned, like a character from a book. She had such a quiet rightness to her, Alex wouldn't feel comfortable going up to her and saying, "Why do you always wear a hat?"

Eddie had speculated that she might be bald, but

with sidelong glances at her, Alex could see that her mass of curly, reddish brown hair sprang from her own scalp.

Candy seemed to know her. "Me and Gwen are old friends, aren't we?" he asked the girl. Because Candy had to be verbal instead of physical, he had become adept at moving right into a girl's territory. He had a style of verbal nudging and teasing that quickly established an easy relationship. "Gwen worked at the Children's Hospital this summer while I was there."

"I didn't work, like really work, there. I was a candy striper is all," she said. Her dark-fringed gray eyes opened wide at Alex. He felt dizzy, as though he were losing his balance.

"I thought you had forgotten me, Candy," she continued.

"Never. Did you get a transfer into here? Let's see your schedule now." Candy reached for the slip of paper and studied it. "What did you change?"

"Math. They put me in another math class, so they had to change some other classes, so here I am." She swept a look back at the teacher and said, "We'd better start writing on this. What are you putting on your questionnaire, Candy?" Her voice was soft. It didn't lift the terrible weight pressing down on Alex, but for a while it did make him forget the reason.

"I'm going to be a stand-up comedian," Candy said. "Honest. That's what I'm putting down."

She giggled with a little burble and raised an eyebrow. "Miss Jernigan said to be realistic."

"I am realistic," Candy said. "If I put down truck driver or football coach, that's not realistic."

Gwen drew the corner of her mouth back into her cheek in a quirky smile that fascinated Alex.

"What are you putting down, Gwen?" Candy asked.

"If you're going to put down the truth about what you want to do, I am, too. I think I'll put down two things. I want to be a poet and a diviner. A diviner. I wouldn't tell anyone else this because they'd just laugh." She slitted her eyes and gave menacing looks to both of them, daring them to laugh.

"So, what's a diviner?" Candy asked.

"A diviner predicts the future and figures out what is the best decision to make. Like, in the old days, Alexander the Great had diviners to tell him which direction to lead his army."

Alex glowed from the sound his name made in her mouth.

"How did the diviner know?"

Alex chewed on his pencil and listened.

"Well, he would sacrifice a goat or a chicken or some animal and look at its liver," Gwen said. Her face was quite serious until she realized the opening she had given Candy.

He let out a suppressed whoop. "Isn't that going to be a messy job? You could just go to Safeway and buy chicken livers. 'Let me have a pound of chicken livers, please. I want to read the future.' " Candy spoke in a high-pitched little-girl's voice.

"Shut up, Candy," Gwen said. She grinned ruefully;

she should have known better than try to be serious with him. She gave Alex her quirky smile. "Alex isn't laughing at me."

Alex ducked his head and started writing on the form in front of him.

Miss Jernigan stopped by their cluster of desks. "How are we doing here? Remember, for any career choice you make, you should list educational requirements, and how you expect to fill these. Use the books on the cart over there to estimate future salary, cost of education, and cost of equipment if you're going to be a doctor or plumber."

She looked over Candy's shoulder. "A stand-up comedian. I see." She looked at Candy. Her face was serious but with just a little smile. They seemed to have a communications wavelength that wasn't accessible to anyone else. "How are you going to prepare for this career, Candy?"

"I watch a lot of TV, Miss."

"You may have trouble researching job requirements and so on, Candy," Miss Jernigan said.

"Can I use *People* magazine as a resource, Miss?"

The teacher's eyebrow rose a skeptical millimeter, then hitched up another notch when she looked at Gwen's paper. "You're going to be a poet and diviner, Gwen?" Miss Jernigan shook her head. "I didn't know we had diviners in the twentieth century."

"Yes, Miss Jernigan. You've heard of water dowsers. They're diviners. In the newspaper every New Year's there are people who make predictions for the year. They're diviners."

"What methods are you expecting to use?" the teacher asked, falling back on her assignment questions.

"The diviners in the old days used animal entrails," Gwen said.

"Entails? End tails?" Candy hooted.

Miss Jernigan very patiently explained what entrails were.

"Chicken livers," Candy interjected.

"Yes, livers are part of the entrails."

Gwen threw him a firm-mouthed look. "Maybe I'll use cards or dice. Julius Caesar threw dice to see if he should cross the Rubicon and lead his army into Rome. I suppose I should train to be a diviner just like any other job."

"I'm almost afraid to ask what occupation you're interested in, Alex. Please say you'd like to be a truck driver or football coach." She looked at his paper, which had only his name, class period, and one line filled in. "*Mm*, trapper. What have you found out about this occupation? Are there many people employed in trapping?"

"No, Ma'am," Alex said. His nose and throat were clogged up by his cold. His voice sounded rusty and far away. "According to what I read, lots of people do it part-time. But there are some men who do it full-time. Like on contract, when coyotes are killing sheep. And in Alaska, there are lots of trappers."

"And Gwen can use all the livers in her job." Candy giggled again.

"What kind of education would you need, Alex?"

"None, Ma'am. I can quit school when I'm sixteen and just start."

"Wouldn't you be more successful if you studied biology or game management or something like that?"

"I don't think so. I think you just learn by doing."

Miss Jernigan's eyes glazed for just a second. She said, "I'm trying to help you people out of childhood into adult reality. Your future is going to be here sooner than you think." Then she said in a lighter voice, "Doesn't anyone want to be a rock star anymore? Whatever happened to the old fantasies?"

Trying to pull it back together, she said to all the class, "Let's get the ball in play here. On the final page of this form, I want you to write what you think you'll be doing ten years from now. What kind of job you'll have, where you'll be living, what you'll use for transportation, what you'll wear, what you'll eat.

"Get working, everyone. The time clock is running out." Miss Jernigan used sports vocabulary so much that Candy called her Coach behind her back. She hurried to a back corner where a flick football game had started in Buddy Jack's group. The folded-paper football zinged off a desk amid loud guffaws. The teacher confiscated it.

Gwen wrote rapidly for some time. Then she looked up and leaned toward Alex. She said, "You like the outdoors?"

"Yes," he whispered back.

"Me too. I hike and backpack a lot with my mother and our dog."

She concentrated on her writing again. When she

lifted her head and looked at Alex full face, the rim of her hat was a halo around her hair. "Is it your friend who's lost?" she asked softly.

Alex nodded. The weight settled into his body again. The far edges of his eyes were stretched to tearing. He wondered how he could bear so much weight and feel hollow at the same time.

"I'm sorry," she whispered.

"How simple it sounds," he thought. "She said she's sorry. She's the only person I've talked to since Friday who seems to know how I'm feeling."

Class time was running out. Departure phase took over. Without being asked for them, students held out their papers to Miss Jernigan. Desks were dragged back into careless rows. Students stacked their books on the desks and leaned their elbows on them.

Alex took Candy's briefcase and said, "I'll see you in the cafeteria. Are you buying lunch?"

"Yeah."

"Me too. We didn't have any bread at home."

"May I sit with you, too?" Gwen asked. Alex was surprised. He didn't remember seeing her in the lunchroom before.

"Sure," he said. "I have to go to my locker first, and to Candy's locker."

When Candy handed his paper to Miss Jernigan, Alex saw her flip to the last page. It was blank. Candy hadn't written any prediction of what he'd be doing ten years from now. She gave Candy an appraising look and she wasn't smiling. That pulse of communication passed between them again.

• • • Chapter Nine

IN THE CAFETERIA, Alex carried both his tray and Candy's. They saw Gwen waving to them from the end of one of the long folding tables where she sat alone.

They advanced through waves of talking and shouting. The sound reverberated through the high-ceilinged, tile-floored room. Alex liked walking through the crowd in Candy's wake. Rather than following a cripple, it was like being in the retinue of a king. Most of the students knew Candy — knew that his bones were so fragile that the most innocent jostling might break a leg or an arm and put him back in the hospital. They opened a way before him. Candy proceeded through the crowd like a very democratic king, with his *thunk-swoosh* gait. Letting go of a crutch, he waved to one friend, did a low high-five with another. He was the only one in the crowd who seemed careless of his safety.

They sat down with Gwen. She pulled food — a

sandwich, an apple, carrot sticks — from a denim bag.

"That smells good," she said, motioning to the bowls of chili on the trays.

"I hope it is. I'm starved," Alex replied. He still couldn't look directly at her, but at least he said two sentences without having the words come out backward. He was hungry. Boots had forgotten to buy bread or eggs yesterday. For breakfast this morning he had drunk a can of diet Coke and opened a can of creamed corn, which he ate cold, straight from the can. Carefully he grasped his spoon in his rough hand and forced himself to pay attention. He wanted to get the food in his mouth without spilling it down his front like some geek.

"Did you see the TV show about the day after a nuclear attack?" Candy asked.

"Yes. It was the assignment in my Social Studies class. Do you have Rinehart, too?" Gwen said.

"Yeah. Pretty real, wasn't it? All those bodies. It was worse than looking at pictures of automobile wrecks."

This wasn't what Alex wanted to hear. Almost constantly, he was haunted by the thought of Eddie lying injured on the mountain.

Awkwardly, he turned the conversation to Gwen. "Have you ever tried predicting anything?" he asked.

"Sort of. Where my grandparents live, in Colorado, there's a man who dowses for water. He says he thinks I have the gift. You know, you use a forked stick. I could really feel it moving. That's like prediction, in a way. Saying, if you dig here, I predict you'll find water." Gwen smiled as though she wouldn't blame them if they didn't believe any of it.

Alex realized there were students at the table turning curious eyes toward them. He tried to ignore them, tune them out. He leaned toward Gwen. He didn't want to be overheard, didn't want to feed the curiosity he could feel directed toward himself. But he had to know something. "Have you ever predicted if someone is alive or dead?"

Candy stopped eating and leaned forward also. His chin just barely cleared the table beside his tray.

Gwen looked Alex full in the face. Her lower lip hung loose, showing her small teeth. She flushed a little and dropped her eyes to her sandwich. "No. Just little things. Like what we're going to have for dinner or what grade I'll make on a test," she said.

"But," Candy said, "you might already know something about those things. Like if you study for a test, you'll know if you're going to do good."

"I know," Gwen said. "But I've done a lot of reading about the old days. Some of those diviners had clues, too, I think. They said that the gods decided the future and the gods decided which way the dice should land. If someone followed the dice, like Caesar, and won big, the people said the gods liked him. If someone followed the dice and lost, people said the gods were punishing the person or the signs weren't read right. So, the diviners probably knew a lot about the situation, and the chances of success. But, see, if they were wrong, they could blame the gods." Gwen slowly ate the last corner of her sandwich.

"Well, do you think you could predict if someone was alive and could be found?" Alex was more insistent.

"I don't know. I suppose I could try." Again, she turned her intense gray eyes on Alex. "You don't really know, do you?" she asked. "You think your friend may be dead on the mountain. Then you think maybe he ran away from home. You don't know what to do."

That was exactly the way Alex felt. But he hadn't been able to put it into words even to himself. He looked at her with awe as though she truly had divined what he felt.

"Hey, on TV, I saw in Chicago, or someplace, where this little kid was lost. The police called a — what do they call them — a psychic to tell them where the kid was," Candy said.

"Did it work?" Alex asked.

"I don't remember," Candy said. He began to eat his fruit cup.

Feeling someone touch the back of his chair, Alex jerked around, startled. He was looking up into Buddy Jack's face — a face as ruddy as Alex's, but beefy, with blond stubble on the jowls. His attitude suggested intimate friendship with Alex. This was stupid, since he had never spoken to him before. Alex could swear that last Thursday, before Eddie disappeared, Buddy Jack didn't even know that Alex existed.

"Hey, Alex," Buddy Jack said, "that dude, Eddie, what happened to him?"

"I don't know," Alex muttered. He turned back to his tray.

Buddy Jack grabbed him by the shoulder. Some of the other students who hung around with Buddy Jack pressed close. Buddy Jack said, "What happened? You guys get in a fight and you killed him?"

Alex refused to look up even though Buddy Jack's hand squeezed his shoulder.

"You're full of it, Buddy Jack. Go soak your head," Candy yelled.

Gwen looked scared. Her eyes darted around as though looking for help, for a teacher.

Buddy Jack guffawed and squeezed Alex tighter. "You got rid of one greaser, Alex. Maybe you better take care of another one." He left no doubt that he meant Candy.

The events of the last seventy-two hours had kept Alex frustrated and confused. Gwen had called it just right. He didn't know what to do or where to turn.

But this situation now, which Buddy Jack had set up, didn't call for much thinking. In just a warning flicker, he knew that Buddy Jack could beat the living shit out of him. Even so, it was an easy decision. He knew what to do. It was almost with relief that he acted.

Pushing his chair back from the table, he caught Buddy Jack in the legs with it. At the same time Alex rose and smashed his elbow into his stomach.

Even bent over, Buddy Jack was taller than Alex. For just a second, Alex was scared by what he'd let himself in for. He hadn't been in a fight since he was in grade school.

Buddy Jack's fist caught him on the side of the head, right in front of his ear. He staggered. Trays and bowls clattered off the table as he tried to regain his balance.

The encircling students were a blur. Their excited yelling blended above the roar in his ears. Metal chairs were thrown aside, but he and Buddy Jack still crowded together in a clutter of fallen folding chairs and tables.

Alex saw Candy stick out one crutch and bat Buddy Jack in the knees with it. Candy's chair was jerked away from the table. His body hit the floor like a marionette whose strings are dropped. With one leg sprawled to the side, he lay there with an astonished look on his face.

Gwen's scream pierced the hubbub. "Get back, you animals. Get back. He's hurt." She dropped to her knees beside him as though to protect him with her body.

Alex stared at Candy in anguish. Buddy Jack wasn't easily distracted. He swung again and caught Alex in the back, in the kidney. Alex staggered. Hands caught him and pushed him toward Buddy Jack.

"All right. Break it up, break it up," Mr. Plemmy yelled in a drill sergeant's voice. He cleaved his way through the crowd as though he were shoving aside bundles of dirty clothes. From the other side of the circle, a cafeteria worker in a white wraparound apron beat his way through in the same manner.

"You two lads, knock it off," the counselor said.

He grabbed Buddy Jack's shoulders as he bunched up for another swing.

"You," he directed Gwen, "go get the nurse. Don't anyone touch Candy. Leave him alone."

To the cafeteria worker, he said, "Stay with him." He motioned toward Candy.

"You two, come with me." He turned brusquely. A path opened for him. Alex and Buddy Jack followed. Mr. Plemmy didn't even look back. His torso in the tight Western shirt rose above the leather belt like a mottled tree trunk.

Buddy Jack's face was still red. He muttered to his friends, who clapped him on his shoulder as he passed. The little procession made its way out of the cafeteria.

When they got to the counselor's office, there was a note clipped to the door. Mr. Plemmy read it and motioned the boys to sit down. "Wait here," he said. "I have to make a phone call." He went in alone and closed the office door.

Four wooden chairs lined the hall outside his office. Alex waited until Buddy Jack sat in the chair closest to the office door. Then he sat at the end of the row, as far from Buddy Jack as possible.

Buddy Jack's face returned to its usual rosy color. There was a jauntiness to the way he sat with one cowboy-booted foot drawn up across his knee. His hands were behind his head with his elbows spread out to the side. "Taking up as much room as he can," Alex thought. "He's used to being in trouble like this."

Alex's ear burned and he felt it to see if the hotness was caused by blood running out. It wasn't. Now with the adrenalin ebbed away, his cold came back in full force. Groping for a tissue in his pocket, he saw food stains down the front of his camouflage shirt. A bean from the chili was smashed into a buttonhole.

All his misery was back. Multipled. Candy was hurt and it was Alex's fault. Maybe he wouldn't be able to walk at all. Alex knew what scorn he had for wheelchairs. "For old women," he said.

Alex remembered vividly the first time he saw Candy. At the beginning of school when it was still hot, Candy wore a red tank top — a muscle shirt — as did many of the guys. His body was thin and pathetic-looking. At first, Alex was embarrassed for him. Soon he came to admire Candy's guts for daring to be normal, and for using his sense of humor to turn away pity.

Even though Candy wanted to be treated like everyone else, Alex felt guilty because it was his fault Candy had been thrown to the floor during the brawl.

And Gwen. She knew how Alex felt, could put it into words. What would she think now? She wasn't the kind of girl who got mixed up in fights. She probably didn't even stay friendly with guys who got mixed up in fights.

Why hadn't he stayed cool? He could have thought of something else to do besides hitting Buddy Jack in the belly.

No. He couldn't. He couldn't think of anything now. No way out.

··· Chapter Ten

ALEX STOOD UP abruptly, almost knocking over the wood chair. Buddy Jack yelled, "Hey, man, where you going?" It was too loud for Alex's benefit; it was meant to alert Mr. Plemmy. "The man said to stay here," Buddy Jack bellowed.

Not hesitating, Alex strode deliberately down the narrow hall toward his locker.

The broad corridor was almost empty. Only a few students floated around, showing no sense of urgency in getting to their classrooms. Some stood in front of open lockers sorting through litter, looking for a pencil or a book. Office aides, chewing gum furiously, passed with small slips of paper in hand. An overweight boy, his black hair hanging in a curtain over his eyes, sauntered down the row of lockers swatting at each combination lock as he passed.

The metallic din broke through Alex's numbness. It reminded him of the old black-and-white prison movies he had seen on TV. The ones where the guards passed the cell doors, rapping on them with a pipe.

He had to get out of here. He was almost running when he reached his locker and thumbed through the combination. As he grabbed his vest, an old habit of thought nudged him to think of homework. He slammed the locker and shut out the thought.

On Friday, he had been a good student, quiet, but trying to do what was expected of him. Trusting his teachers when they told him what he learned in school was going to help him later in life. Today he could barely have named the classes he was in. Nothing of school had any relevance for him. Not the classes or teachers. Not the sports. None of these different groups of people who liked to label themselves and others: the jocks, the cowboys, the druggies, the ones from the Golden Ghetto with their cars and bright clothes.

The long, fluorescent tubes on the ceiling splayed the green walls and banks of lockers with a cold light, a death-ray kind of light. At the end of the corridor, the double glass doors stood closed. But the sun's light beckoned, promising warmth and reality.

Alex thought, "It was so different when Eddie was here." When school first started, it was exciting moving through this big, crowded school, feeling you were part of the energy. Together they bucked the mob strength as students pushed through the corridors at change of class. They found their way down the maze of corridors together. Cracking the code on their computer-printed schedule, they discovered the other buildings where their classes took them.

Without Eddie, Alex felt overwhelmed by the size of everything. Without a friend, all he could see was the coldness of the school. He was just a number, of interest today because of Eddie's disappearance. Next week, he'd drop back to being just a number again.

Outside the doors, Alex stepped to the side of the entrance and drew a wad of tissues from his pocket. He gave a good blow to his nose and dabbed at his watery eyes. His throat was raw and swollen.

For just a second, Alex thought of going to the nurse's office and getting checked out to go home. Quickly, he rejected the thought. First, the nurse's office was in that same warren where the counselors' offices were. If he went back, he'd risk running into Plemmy. And Buddy Jack.

Second, the nurse probably wouldn't release him unless Boots came for him. He didn't want her coming here and getting mixed up in his school life. She just didn't understand how it was. The way she dressed, they wouldn't even believe she was his mother.

The nurse was busy anyway, he thought, with a guilty click. Candy would be there, lying on one of the small cots. Alex forgot his own swollen miserable head. He wondered how pain was for Candy. Did he hurt more or less than healthy people? His face never showed any sign, not even discomfort. Alex remembered him as he lay sprawled on the cafeteria floor, face red with excitement, eyes wide in astonishment. There was almost a touch of glee, Alex thought. Candy had been floored in a brawl. His disability shielded him from such rowdiness. But he had moved outside that protection both to help Alex and to get his own lick in. Buddy Jack had insulted him with that crack about Mexicans.

If Candy was hurt so badly that he had to go back to the hospital, then Alex wouldn't have any friends at school. Gwen hardly counted as a friend since he hadn't even talked to her until today.

Alex fought down an urge to go back and find out if Candy had broken any bones. He just couldn't go back in that building. He'd call Candy later.

Walking slowly, Alex left the stony gray building with its vertical slit windows. Suddenly, in front of him, the concrete sidewalk was flooded with girls in black shorts and yellow shirts with big black numbers. They were moving toward the bus waiting by the curb.

"Volleyball? Basketball?" Alex wondered. He didn't know. Organized sports — who was playing on what team against whom — just didn't have anything to do with his school life. He and Eddie lived in a world where what was being served in the cafeteria was more interesting than whether a team would get to the state finals.

To avoid the girl athletes, he stepped off the sidewalk onto the bare earth. The walks radiated from the main building. The shrubs planted in rows alongside them didn't have much effect on the bleakness of the sandy grounds. The grayish plants looked tough, defensive. Gum wrappers and bits of shiny plastic caught in their stiff leaves and littered the shallow cracked-mud irrigation basins in which they stood.

Alex had never left the school grounds on foot be-

100

fore. He and Eddie always rode the bus home. He knew a gate opened in the chain link fence onto Juan Tabo Boulevard. Away from the sidewalk, he zigzagged through the parking lot crowded with the students' cars and trucks. Just last week, he and Eddie had fantasized about the day they would drive onto this parking lot in their new vehicles.

There were a few other students outside. Some boy-girl couples were pressed into inconspicuous corners. Others walked purposefully toward their cars — probably hurrying to a job. Alex knew this school had work-study programs for seniors.

In contrast, there was a clot of hangers-on by the gate. Neither in school nor quite out of it, they leaned against the chain links, standing on one leg with the other foot angled back to push against the fence. A cigarette passed from hand to hand.

"Hey, man," one yelled at Alex as he went through the gate. In stringy hair and a long black raincoat, he held the butt of the cigarette between two grimy fingers. "Hey, man," he yelled again. "Ain't you . . .?"

"Say, where you going so fast, dude?" yelled another. "They know, they know," Alex thought. "Somehow, even this bunch knows about Eddie's disappearance." He got through the gate and started down the street.

• • •

It was a long walk home. When he got there, Boots's car was gone. Monday was her day off. Usually she went to dance class on Monday afternoons.

The trailer was stifling hot. Boots had forgotten to turn off the heat when she left. Alex opened the refrigerator and closed it. He was hungry, but there were only a couple of diet Cokes in there.

No bread, no leftovers. If he didn't shop, there would be no dinner this evening, no breakfast and no lunch tomorrow.

He got some money from the baking powder can that was Boots's bank account and headed for the supermarket.

He pushed his half-full cart to the bread racks last. From the corner of his eye he saw a woman approaching from the bakery. Eddie's mother, Mrs. Rodriguez, had a white apron on so that it covered most of her body. Flour powdered her forearms. Her hair was tied back under a white cap. In her hand she held an empty tray.

"Alex, I want to see you. It's time for my break. Meet me outside by the back entrance," she said.

Excitement rose in Alex. She must have some news about Eddie. Impatiently, he waited his turn in the express check-out line and hurried outside, past the loading dock.

When he got to the big dumpsters, he saw Mrs. Rodriguez standing beside a closed steel door. She had put on a sweater. Her arms were folded across her chest.

When he got close, Alex could see that she didn't want to tell him anything. Her face was gray and she looked more tired than Alex remembered. "Alex," she said in a pleading voice, "why don't you tell the police what happened to Eddie?"

Alex started to leave without saying anything, but something about her misery held him. He would try to say it so she could understand.

"Eddie's my best friend, Mrs. Rodriguez. I told the police everything I know. I don't know where he is. I think he's still up there on the mountain."

They both looked at the purple-gray mass of granite to the east. Beyond the electric wires and tier after tier of houses, the mountains rose. High, jagged ridges. Forbidding cold flanks.

"If I could just know. Maybe I could get some sleep, some rest. Tell me," she pleaded.

"But I don't know. I think he's up there, but I couldn't find him. The search party couldn't find him. I swear — I don't know."

"How could he be alive if he's up there all this time?"

"He's probably not alive," Alex said. He felt his eyes and nose moisten.

She narrowed her black eyes and hissed, "You know. You did something to him. Maybe killed him. Then left him. Now you torture me by not telling. You try to make the police think he ran away. My boy wouldn't run away. He's not that kind. You did something. Tell me."

Alex turned and walked away. He heard the metal clang as she went inside.

When he was on the broad cross-town street, he

looked at the mountains again. Cold, seemingly life-less. From here a person would never guess that there were trees and water. Sandia — someone had said it was Spanish for watermelon mountains, named for their pink color when the evening sun hit them a certain way. To Alex, they didn't look like watermelons. They looked deadly.

At the trailer, he stowed the few groceries away. He found himself looking at a can of tomato soup for a long time. "Decide," he thought. "Yes or no. No. And no sandwich either." He poured some milk and carried it to the couch. Clicked on the TV. Laughter, loud voices poured over him. Finally, realizing he wasn't listening, he turned it off.

With the empty glass in his hand, he wandered into the kitchen and looked out the window.

Something caught his eye. Something between the weeds and the old tires at the back of the Rodriguez trailer. It was a bike. It looked like Eddie's old one. Maybe Mrs. Rodriguez had known something else about Eddie's disappearance. She just hadn't told Alex.

The door of the Rodriguez trailer opened slowly. Deenie backed out of the door, carefully closing it behind her as if she didn't want to disturb someone inside. She was dressed in her usual tight-fitting black jeans and boots, with a denim jacket. She carried a large denim pouch bag.

She shook her hair back from her face. Slowly, she surveyed the neighborhood. Alex saw that her make-up couldn't hide the damage done to her face. Her upper lip was puffed up. There was an angry red welt beside her right eye.

Alex wondered if her mother knew she wasn't in school.

He opened the door and said softly, "Deenie."

She turned, startled, her eyes big and afraid. When she saw Alex, she frowned and put her finger to her lips. He motioned her to come to the stoop of his trailer, but she went around to the side, out of sight of her own home. Alex rushed down the steps after her.

"Hey, Deenie, hold up," he said, and she stopped to wait for him.

When he faced her, Alex saw the same strung-out tiredness that was in her mother's face. On her thin face, the size of her lip was alarming. Her old sauciness was gone and her eyes wouldn't stay on his, but kept sliding off. "Is that Eddie's bike over by your trailer?" he asked.

"There's a bike. The police brought it. They said it was found in the Embudito Flood Ditch. They asked if it was Eddie's. I don't know. Mom doesn't know. We didn't pay any attention to Eddie's bike. Mando said it was Eddie's, so the police left it."

"I'll look at it. After a while. Maybe I can tell. Did the police say who found it?"

"Some kids up there. They took it home and their dad called the police."

"How'd you get the fat lip?" Alex asked.

"What're you doing home?" she countered. She sounded sullen.

"I got into a fight," he said. He cupped his hand

around his ear. It didn't feel so bad now. Most of the heat was gone, but it felt puffed up, like a boxer's.

"Who?" she asked almost mechanically.

"Buddy Jack. That's all the name I know. You probably don't know him."

"Did you fight about a girl?" she asked. Her head was lowered and draperies of black hair covered most of her face. She studied some gravel she was stirring with the toe of her black boot.

"No. It was about Eddie," Alex said. He flushed as he remembered what Buddy Jack had said. He hoped Deenie wouldn't ask. She didn't. She just let it drop.

"Gotta go, Redhead," she said. Her words sounded like the old Deenie, but there was no snap to them.

She went toward the back of Alex's trailer and slipped behind the next one in line. Alex guessed she would squeeze through the break in the fence and go into the asphalt parking lot of the next-door apartments.

She didn't want to be seen, Alex thought. As he went back to the front of his trailer, he studied the one she had just come from. It was quiet. No curtain was parted suspiciously.

He started back to examine the half-hidden bike. When he saw Paco Rodriguez's truck parked on the other side of their trailer, he changed his mind. No need to get him stirred up about something like that. He wondered if the battered white truck had been parked there when he went by on his way to and from the supermarket. He'd been so wrapped in his own thoughts he hadn't noticed.

• • • Chapter Eleven

A LEX SLUMPED on the couch in the darkening afternoon, neither asleep nor fully awake. The empty milk glass stood on the end table. The trailer had cooled down, but it didn't matter. His cold and the aspirins he took made his body indifferent to the temperature. Hot, cold. Indoors, outdoors. It didn't matter.

He tried to rerun his last memory of Eddie. Eddie hung suspended in that golden explosion of leaves, his clothes black against the white trunks of the aspens. "Hey, man," he said in his raspy voice, "find me." But Alex couldn't see his face now. Also, the memory got shorter every time he replayed it. Just went zipping by in fast forward.

Alex fought for control over that image. It was his last look at Eddie. Another image tried to push into Alex's head — a picture of Eddie sprawled face-up on a sharp incline of jumbled boulders. Blood ran from his mouth just as it had from the trapped ground squirrel.

"No," Alex said to himself. "I won't even think it. It's not true. I didn't see Eddie like that. No matter what the police think. No matter what Eddie's mother thinks. I didn't kill Eddie. I didn't hurt him."

He tried to reconstruct Eddie again. His face came, the skin crinkled around his dark eyes, the red welt on his cheekbone. Alex heard his whispery voice saying, "Paco decked me, is all."

Unbidden, Deenie's face floated into focus. He heard his own voice asking, "How'd you get the fat lip?"

Alex remembered the evenings when he had been alone and thinking of the Chavez kids next door. He had imagined the fat smell of taco shells cooking, the warmth of kids packed around the dining room table, a father at one end, a mother at the other. Everything in this picture was missing from his own life. Now that he knew there was brutality and fear in that next-door trailer, he was not so eager to trade his loneliness for life like that.

The phone rang. Candy's voice was on the other end. "Hey, that was something today, huh?" He sounded ebullient. "Did you see me whack that bastard in the legs?"

"Yeah. You did. I saw you. Uh, Candy, did you get hurt? Like break anything?"

"Naw," Candy said, as though he were as sturdy as any varsity athlete. "Just bruised a little. What

108

happened to you? Did Plemmy suspend you? What about Buddy Jack?"

"I don't know. I cut out. You know — left," Alex replied.

"What do you mean, you left? You can't just walk out when they take you to the office."

"I did. Plemmy left Buddy Jack and me sitting outside his office. I couldn't take it. Plemmy or that big mouth, Buddy Jack. I walked home."

"Boy, you've got trouble tomorrow."

"I might not come tomorrow. I might not come back at all."

"You're only fifteen. You can't drop out."

"I can't take that Plemmy guy. He's so phony. He had me in the office once already today. First period. Tried to pretend he didn't even know about Eddie. I think he was trying to get me to confess."

"Confess what?" Candy asked.

"Confess that I killed Eddie. That we had a fight or something."

"He watches too many detectives on TV," Candy said in his thin voice.

"Then the juvenile officer — I forgot to tell you about her."

"Her? A woman? Was she pretty?"

"Cut it out. She was pretty old. She used to be a school counselor in the valley and knew Eddie's brother. She acted like she thought Eddie might have cut out of here to go into drugs or something."

"Eddie wouldn't do that," Candy said.

"I know. Eddie knows about prison because Johnny's there. He wouldn't take a chance on ending up there."

Candy asked, "Was Eddie's brother a dealer? I was in Children's Hospital when he was sent up."

"Naw. Eddie says he was just driving a car that was down at the border to pick up some stuff. The other guys ran off and left Johnny to take the heat when the narcs caught them."

"Didn't Eddie ever try anything, not even grass?"

"He said he didn't, and said he wouldn't. Said he wasn't going to have anything to do with substances."

Alex tried to recall what else he was going to tell Candy, see what ideas Candy might have. He remembered. "She asked if there were any cars or trucks parked at the trailhead when I came out Friday. I can't remember."

They both thought about this.

Alex added, "I saw Eddie's sister after I got home, and she said the police brought a bike to their house. They think it might be Eddie's. Eddie's stepdad is in the trailer and I think he's drunk. So I had to sneak over to look at it. I think it's Eddie's. I can't be sure. Eddie's bike was pretty beat-up but this one is more beat-up, and the handlebars and seat are gone."

"If Eddie came down from the mountain and didn't ride his bike someplace," Candy reasoned, "maybe he left in a car."

"You mean, maybe someone snatched him? They only steal little kids," Alex protested.

"Maybe it was someone he knew. Maybe they were supposed to wait for him." Candy suggested.

"Aw, that's dumb, man. Nobody knew we were going to ditch school and go on the mountain. Nobody knew when we'd be back. Nobody even knew Eddie might come down by himself. What would they do if I was with him?"

"Don't get excited, Alex. I'm just thinking. Eddie could have set it up."

"You sound like Plemmy," Alex scoffed. "You know Eddie better than that. He doesn't think ahead to set things up. He just does them. He couldn't fool me, anyway, if he tried to trick me that way."

"Well, he fooled you one way, guy," Candy said.

"Yeah? How's that?"

"You don't know where he is."

Alex was silent for a long time. Then slowly he said, "Yeah, I do. In a way. I think he's still up there. He fell over some cliff or into some old mine shaft no one knows about."

"Then, he's . . ."

"Yeah. I think he's dead."

The word hung between them, in the phones, in the crackling wire, in the air.

. . .

"In the evening, that's when the fever's always the highest. That's what Mom used to say," Boots said.

Wrapped in a blanket but still shivering, Alex thought about Mom. When he used to be sick with a cold or the flu, he just gave up and put his life into her hands. Like one of those pupas in an anthill that the ant nurses feed and clean and move if the anthill is disturbed. Mom took care of everything and he got well.

Boots didn't feel his forehead to take his temperature the way Mom did. She made him hold the thermometer in his mouth, then made him hold it again after she misread it. Whatever it read, he felt awful.

With her blond hair pulled high in a ponytail, wearing Lycra tights and a long sweater stretched to her thighs, Boots looked like a teenager, the way Alex first remembered her when she drove from Albuquerque to Las Cruces to visit. She'd take Alex in her Maverick to the Sonic Drive-in and let him drink Cokes while she talked with friends from high school days.

"Here," she said now, "drink this. You're supposed to drink lots of fluids." She thrust a can of lemon soda in his hands.

She set up a TV tray beside him and another for herself at the other end of the couch. On each she placed a plate with a slice of pizza. Beside Alex's tray she put a mug of hot tea.

"So, what happened at school today?" she asked brightly. Usually Alex ate dinner alone because Boots had to leave for work at 4 P.M. He sometimes thought, during their few meals together, that she made conversation with him the way she did with the customers she served at the bar.

"Well, Eddie, you know, there was . . . " Alex's throat was raw and he didn't want to talk, but he tried again. "Plemmy — he's a counselor — called me in first period to talk about my ditching school on Friday. Then there was a policewoman, and she asked more questions about Eddie."

"You didn't get much studying done, huh?"

"There was this guy in the cafeteria, a big guy, and I got in a fight with him," Alex said. He decided not to tell Boots what Buddy Jack had said. "So Plemmy took us to his office, but I felt awful. So I left and came home."

Boots held her pizza away from her face and frowned at him. "Whoah, buster. Too much here. Did you check out of school? You can't just walk out, can you? When I was in school, you couldn't just leave."

Alex didn't say anything, and she went on. "Why didn't you go to the nurse's office? They could have called me. I was home until two o'clock."

Then she sorted back through his terse account. "What were you fighting about? Who started it? I can't believe it. You never got into trouble before."

"I guess I hit him first," Alex said. "They'll probably call you. You'll probably have to go to school."

"Jeez. I just can't believe it. What got into you? It's this Eddie thing, isn't it? You should never have hung around with him. Mexicans . . . " Apparently she decided Alex looked miserable enough because she broke off and chewed her pizza silently.

By a train of thought that Alex couldn't have followed even if he wasn't sick, Boots began to talk about the bar. "One of my regulars. His name's Oscar something. He comes in two or three times a week. Must not have much money because he just drinks Elkhorn beer. That's the cheapest we have. He was so sad the other day. He's got a son, a grown son. And the son doesn't write, doesn't call. 'Don't even know I'm alive,' Oscar says. His face was so sad, and a tear rolled down across his beard and dropped into his mug of Elkhorn."

Boots smiled a sad, sweet smile at Alex. He thought of grandparents far away in Arizona when he needed them, and a mother who thought a drunk in the bar was sad, but didn't recognize the pain her own son was feeling. He thought about Eddie dying alone, and Candy who had no future. A tear welled out of Alex's eye, trickled down his cheek, and fell into the cup of tea he cradled in both hands. Boots didn't seem to notice.

· · ·

When the phone rang, Boots undoubled from her cross-legged position to answer. She raised a thin eyebrow and smiled a teasing smile at Alex as she handed him the phone. When he heard a girl's voice, he was confused and blushed. He heard, "Alex? This is Gwen. Alex, are you OK?"

"Yeah, I'm all right," Alex said. He was aware that Boots was close, listening.

"I just talked with Candy," she said. "He gave me your number. Gosh. I was scared today. I was afraid Candy'd broken his leg and would have to go back to the hospital."

"Can't the doctors do something to help him?" Alex asked.

"They put rods in his legs. And he does exercises. That's about all. It's called osteogenesis imperfecta. There's no cure."

"Will it . . . how long will he live?"

"I don't know. I just know what I learned this summer at the hospital." Her voice was grave. "You sound like your cold's worse. Candy told me you left school this afternoon."

"Yeah."

"Will you get suspended?"

"I don't know," Alex muttered.

"I'll bring your assignments, if you want. If you're suspended the teachers won't give you credit for your work."

"What's the point of doing it then?" Alex asked.

"They can't keep you from learning. You do the work so you don't get behind, so you can do well on semester tests and so on."

"It doesn't matter," Alex said. "I'm not going to be around long enough for it to matter. Nothing matters."

"You'll feel different when you get over your cold," Gwen said.

"When I get over my cold, Eddie still won't be here."

"Oh, Alex, I'm sorry. Sometimes I'm a Pollyanna. I forget how much you worry about him. You know what you were asking today, about whether I could predict where Eddie could be found and if he was alive?"

"Yeah?" Alex said cautiously. He was very aware of his mother's presence.

"I don't think I can but I'll try. Don't count on it though."

"Well, you seem to know lots of things other people don't know," Alex said.

"I think that's just because I try to be quiet and really listen to what people are saying."

"That makes you different right there," Alex said with a short, barking laugh.

"Are you coming to school tomorrow?" she asked.

"I don't know. Not if I feel like this," Alex said.

"We just have tomorrow and the next day, then Thursday is Thanksgiving."

"Yeah. I know."

"I've got to go now. I've got to feed the dog."

"Well, goodbye." After he hung up, Alex thought he should have thanked her for calling. "Once a geek always a geek," he thought.

. . .

At 10 P.M., Alex heard Boots say, "Hey, lover, it's time to change into your pajamas and get to bed."

"You wake me up to tell me to go to bed," Alex grumbled. He was sweaty and his head was completely clogged up. He worked his knuckles around his eyes to dislodge the crust.

Suddenly he came awake as he heard the TV news announcer: " . . . from their home in the Northeast

Heights. Denise Chavez, an eighth-grader in Grant Middle school, was reported missing by her mother this evening. Denise did not attend school today, and has not been seen by her family since early this morning. In a curious twist to this story, Denise is the sister of Eddie Chavez, who was reported missing this past Friday when he failed to return from a hike in the Sandia Mountains."

On the screen, Alex saw the same picture of the trailer court that had been shown on Sunday. Mrs. Rodriguez stood outside her trailer, her eyes squinting against the bright light. Beside her, Deenie looked straight at the camera.

The announcer hurried on. "Police declined to speculate on whether the two disappearances are connected. They ask anyone who has information about Denise's whereabouts to call the police." He gave a number and then launched into the next story at top speed.

"This morning," Alex thought. "He said her family hasn't seen her since this morning. But she was at the trailer this afternoon. It must have been about 3 P.M. when I saw her leave the trailer."

"Did you hear that?" Boots asked. "Another one. Another one of their kids is missing." She sounded as though Mexicans were especially careless of their children, misplacing them all the time.

"Boots, I wish you'd stop being so prejudiced. They're just people like us, just trying to get along."

Alex started to tell Boots about seeing Deenie, then stopped. If he told Boots, he thought, then he'd have to tell the police. "They haven't believed anything I've said about Eddie. They think I'm lying. They probably think I killed him. If I tell them I'm the last person here at the trailer court to see Deenie, they'll think they have their connection to Eddie's disappearance. The connection: me."

Paco Rodriguez must have been in that trailer this afternoon. His truck was there. And Deenie shut the door carefully as though she didn't want someone inside to hear her. But what could he say? He couldn't say he saw Paco. He couldn't say Paco had been beating on Deenie.

He wasn't going to tell anyone anything. They wouldn't believe him anyway.

• • • Chapter Twelve

A LEX HADNT SET his clock, but he woke up at 6:30 A.M. anyway. He'd been driven out of his sleep by a dream. Not much of it stayed with him — just a feeling of rejection. His friends from his past, from Las Cruces, were in it. They were playing catch, but they wouldn't throw the ball to him. They acted as though they couldn't see him. As though he didn't exist.

Deciding not to go to school was not really a decision. He just didn't have the will to get up and get dressed. Logy from sleep, he was still exhausted because he had waked up frequently: to blow his nose, to find a way to arrange his arms and legs so he didn't ache, to cup his hand over his ear to ease the pain.

Each time he waked, thoughts of Eddie flooded his mind. He fought to keep back the image of Eddie that didn't belong there, the image of Eddie lying on his back with the blood coming from his mouth. He hadn't seen that. It didn't belong there with the true memories.

He dozed off again.

When he heard the knock on the door, it was about 10:30 A.M. and sunshine was streaming in the bedroom window. Hurriedly pulling on his jeans and camouflage shirt, he went to the door in his bare feet. It took him a second to recognize Lily Torres, the juvenile officer who had questioned him yesterday at school. Looking past her, he saw a city police car pulled up beside Boots's old Maverick.

"Good morning, Alex," she said. "May I come in?"

Alex stood aside silently, then closed the door after her. He clawed little chunks of matter from his eyelashes. Feeling guilty because he was found at home on a school day, he buttoned the camouflage shirt clear to his chin. He rolled down the sleeves and buttoned the cuffs, leaving inches of red, weathered wrists showing.

Alex turned his back to her and coughed extravagantly. While he was giving a good blow to his nose, Lily Torres opened her briefcase at the formica-topped table.

"Maybe you'd better put some shoes on, Alex," she reminded him in a soft voice.

When he returned from his bedroom with his untied Reeboks on his feet, she asked, "Is your mother at home? Do you suppose she could join us?"

Obediently, Alex shuffled back to Boots's room and tapped on the door. He called, "Mom," several times. He was, he realized, trying to make the officer think

120

they were a regular family. Hearing no sound, he finally called, "Boots," and heard her say "Ummm?" long-drawn out and like a question.

"Boots, there's somebody here. Get up." The bed creaked and Alex heard silken rustles. When she opened her door, he put his finger on his lips. "It's the police," he said. "Get dressed before you come out."

Smeared eye make-up made her seem more gaunt than she was. Her hair hung raveled out, uncertain. She was tightening the belt on her pink satin wrapper. Confused eyes looked out from under the rounded brows, and her mouth pulled into a sulky, stubborn set.

"Please, Boots," Alex said.

• • •

"She'll just be a few minutes," Alex said to Lily Torres. But he knew better. He could hear the water running in the shower. From shower to dressed and presentable would take Boots a long time.

"Would you like some tea?" Alex asked. He moved slowly, acting out how miserable he felt so Ms. Torres wouldn't expect him to be in school. His mouth was grim from the long night. He wanted to brush his teeth, but he couldn't do that with Boots in the bathroom. Maybe the tea would wash away some of the bad taste.

"Your cold's still pretty bad, isn't it?" Lily Torres asked.

"Yeah. That's why I decided to stay home today."

Alex didn't sit at the table, but stood by the window. The officer didn't seem uncomfortable sitting by herself. As she lifted the mug of tea to her lips, the steam fogged her glasses.

"What classes are you taking at school?"

Alex mumbled through the list.

"Do they still have mock trials in the ninth grade? I remember when I was in high school, I got to be the district attorney, and I was so nervous." Lily Torres talked on, telling Alex how she grew up in the South Valley and went to the old Albuquerque High School.

Alex listened for the shower to be turned off. This empty time was dangerous for him. Ms. Torres's voice, her manner, invited confidence. He stiffened his lips to keep from saying anything about Deenie. Nor would he volunteer any information about Eddie. If the police had believed him to start with, they might have found Eddie.

The scent of cosmetics preceded Boots into the living room and kitchen. Her hair was a mass of long, springy ringlets, and she had put on a lean, blue pullover and jeans. With bright eyes and her mouth ready to smile, she saw Lily Torres sitting at the kitchen table. Not a flicker of disappointment crossed her face when she realized the officer was a woman.

After introducing herself, Boots eased into a kitchen chair, crossed her legs, and kicked her booted foot around in little circles. Smiling gently at Alex, she asked if he would bring her a cup of tea.

Ms. Torres got out her yellow pad of lined paper. "I just want to ask both of you some questions about

Denise Chavez. Mrs. Ashley — is it Mrs.? OK. Ms. Ashley, were you here at home yesterday? Um. Part of the time? When were you here?"

"Yesterday? Monday? That's my day off. Let's see. I slept until about eleven. You know, I work nights, so I always sleep until eleven or twelve. Even on my day off. I don't change my schedule. It's hard on my sytem to change my wake-sleep cycle." Boots frowned. "So I was out of it until about eleven. After I showered and dressed, I left about noon."

"Did you see anyone or hear anything around the Rodriguez trailer while you were here?"

"No, it was quiet as the grave around here. It usually is quiet in the daytime after the kids have gone to school and everyone has gone to work. It's about the only good thing about this dump. I can get enough sleep."

"When did you return home?"

"About two. I came back to get my exercise clothes. I have dance class at two-thirty," Boots answered.

"Did you see anyone around the Rodriguez trailer at that time?"

"I don't know. Let me think. No kids." Thinking, Boots frowned, pulling her brows down, making her eyes look guarded like Alex's. Suddenly her face shook off its contortions. "Yeah. Him. Chavez. Whatever his name is — Rodriguez. Yeah, he was in his white truck. Followed me into the trailer court. Crowding me, like he was in a hurry. I've got to go slow over those bumps out there, because my shocks are shot. He was right on my tail, pushing."

123

"Do you mean Francisco Rodriguez?" Lily Torres stared intently through her oversize glasses.

"Yeah. I guess. The man who lives over there."

"Did you see him go into the trailer? Or did you speak with him?"

"No. I wasn't watching him. But before I could get my door unlocked, I heard him slam his trailer door."

Alex turned his back, ostensibly to blow his nose again. He was surprised. He hadn't thought about Boots knowing anything about Deenie, or Paco Rodriguez.

"Now, Alex. If I could ask you some questions. Why don't you sit down here, too?" Lily Torres turned an expectant face to Alex and he sat down.

"Mr. Plemmy says you left school early yesterday afternoon. What time did you leave?"

"I don't know. Plemmy knows. Right after lunch. After he took me to his office," Alex said. He kept his eyes down. Out of sight, under the table, his fingers were knit tightly together.

"What did you do after you left school?"

"Walked home. It's about three miles."

"Did you come straight home?"

"Yeah."

"Was your mother here when you got home?"

"No."

"What did you do then?"

"I got some money and my bike and went to the store to buy some groceries."

"Careful, now," Alex told himself. "There's no reason to mention Mrs. Rodriguez, unless she asks."

124

"What time did you get home from the store?" Lily Torres asked.

"I don't know. It was still too early for school to be out."

"Your school's out at three-thirty?"

"Yeah." Alex was not saying much, but the policewoman's pen scratched as she looped her big script across the yellow legal pad.

"So, do you think you got here the first time before 2 P.M. and after the grocery store you were back here before three-thirty?"

"Yeah. I guess so."

"Did you see anyone around the Rodriguez trailer?" Lily Torres stopped writing and looked straight at him, straight into his eyes. Alex shifted his gaze to the tabletop.

"No," he mumbled.

"What makes you think you got back here before three-thirty?" Ms. Torres asked.

"Uhh. There weren't any kids around — the streets or anyplace. And the TV. I turned on the TV. I could tell from the program."

"What program was it?"

"Uhh. I don't remember now. But I knew then. I knew it was on before three-thirty."

"Did you see Denise yesterday?"

"Maybe I saw her in the morning. Waiting for the bus. I don't remember."

"Did you see Denise yesterday afternoon after you came home from school?"

"Hold on, officer," Boots said. She was leaning forward with one arm stuck out in front of Alex — the way mothers, when they're driving, stick an arm in front of little children in the front seat to keep them from shooting into the dashboard. "Alex has already answered that question. It sounds like you're picking on him. Just like the police did about Eddie. You can't hold him responsible if that family keeps losing their kids."

"Sorry," Lily Torres said. "We're just trying to locate the kids. Find out who saw them last and so on. Did you know that seven kids disappeared in Albuquerque last year? Seven kids gone without a trace."

"Disappeared?" Alex asked. In his mind, he saw seven kids, one after the other, leap into the air. At the top of the leap, each one disappeared in a *poof* of gold dust. Just like a magic act.

The interruption gave Alex time to think. Maybe Ms. Torres already knew he had talked with Deenie. Maybe someone saw him, the way Boots had seen Paco Rodriguez. What difference did it make anyway? He couldn't believe that Deenie was in danger. Would Lily Torres believe him?

"So," the officer turned back to Alex, "did you see Denise yesterday afternoon?"

"Yeah," he said and heard Boots draw her breath in sharply.

"Tell me about it, Alex."

Alex told her. About the sneaky way Deenie came out the door, about the big denim pouch, about going outside to ask about the bike.

"How did she seem?"

"What do you mean?"

"Was she like her usual self? What did she seem like?"

"She wasn't like usual. She was like . . . like, scared," Alex answered.

"Did she tell you what was wrong?"

"No."

"Did she say anything about why she was home from school?"

"No. She said something. I forget what. Then she sneaked behind our trailer on this side." Alex motioned to the area away from the Rodriguez trailer.

"Do you know where she went?"

"No."

"Do you know any of her friends?"

"No. Just the kids she hangs around with here."

"Did Denise come inside this mobile home?" Ms. Torres asked.

Before Alex could answer, Boots interjected again. "What are you getting at? Alex said he went outside to talk with her. Why don't you ask those Mexicans what's going on in that trailer? What makes their kids run away from home?"

Lily Torres didn't give any sign that she was offended by Boots's spitting out "those Mexicans" like a dirty word. "You think they ran away from home?" she asked Boots quietly.

"Sure they did," Boots rattled out like machine-gun fire. "They're someplace with relatives. You know those Mexicans. They've got so many relatives, they probably forgot to tell the police about them all. Those kids are someplace safe, laughing about the stuff on TV, about missing children."

"Eddie's not laughing," Alex said. "Eddie's up on the mountain somewhere. He never came off."

"You don't think Eddie's a runaway, then?" Miss Torres asked.

"No. Eddie's dead," he replied.

"What makes you think that?"

"I've told you. I've told the other police officer. No one believes me."

"Tell me again," Lily Torres suggested.

"No," Alex said. He pushed away from the table and stood up. He was going to go to his room.

"Wait, Alex," she said. "You seem very sure that Eddie's dead. There's only one way you can be absolutely sure. Why don't you tell me all that you know?"

As Alex turned away and went down the narrow hall, he heard Boots's staccato speech. "I don't like what you're saying, officer. You'd better have some proof . . . " Alex closed his bedroom door. He could hear only voices, no words, after that.

· · · Chapter Thirteen

WEDNESDAY MORNING just before noon, after she had her shower and was dressed, Boots came into the living room. Alex sat huddled on the couch. A booklet entitled *Guide to the Mammals of the Sandia Mountains* lay unopened beside him. The brightness was gone from his hair and it stuck out in clumps made from sweaty contact with the pillow. When he finally raised his head to look at his mother, his eyes were dull and lifeless.

"What's the matter, babe? Isn't your cold getting any better?" she asked. She laid her hand tentatively on his forehead.

"I'm OK. I just didn't feel like going to school."

"Well, tomorrow's Thanksgiving. There's probably not much going on in your classes today anyway. Do you want me to go to school and get the assignments that you missed this week?"

"It doesn't matter. I might not go back to school. I might just quit."

"What do you mean — quit? You can't quit. You're not old enough to quit, not old enough to hold a job. Jeez, what do you think you'll do if you quit?" Boots stood with arms akimbo, waiting for an answer.

"Just quit." Alex spoke slowly, as though he didn't even have the strength or the interest to shape words.

"That's silly," Boots said. "When you feel better, you'll see what a bad idea quitting is."

"It's not the same without Eddie."

"You've got other friends. How about Candy? And the girl who called you the other day? What's her name?"

"Candy can't get out and do anything. He's got something wrong with his bones. He's going to die, too. It isn't fair." Alex didn't want to explain about Gwen, so he ignored that part of Boots's question.

"No, life's not always fair. But what's all this talk about dying? You're just making yourself morbid. Eddie's not dead."

"Yes, he is," Alex insisted. His mouth set in a stubborn line. "I wish people would — you know, like when there's an accident or something, then there's a funeral. Everyone is sad, but it's like saying goodbye. Then it's over."

"But Alex, you don't know for sure where Eddie is." Boots watched Alex closely. His mouth was still clamped stubbornly. "The police don't know where he is. His family doesn't know where he is. He's gonna turn up. Maybe Deenie, too. Maybe they're at the same place. Maybe they're together. Have you thought of that?"

130

"Eddie's dead. I know it. He's not coming back."

"Alex, you're just making trouble for yourself. Just being human means that you'll have enough miseries in life without making up new ones for yourself. Now, that's enough of that kind of talk. Have you had breakfast? How about lunch?" Boots's voice went up to the cheery level used by TV sitcom mothers.

Alex declined.

"Say, how about getting off that couch and taking a shower? Wash your hair. You'll feel better. And change clothes. You've worn that shirt so long it stinks."

The too-tight camouflage shirt was buttoned at the neck and cuffs. Alex stared at his hands and didn't seem to hear her.

· · ·

The phone rang for a long time. Echoes of its past ringing hung in the air before Alex unfolded from the couch to answer it.

"Hey, man, why didn't you come to school today?" Alex heard Candy ask.

"I don't know. I don't feel so good."

"Buddy Jack didn't get suspended. He was right there in Careers class. He's loud-mouthed, like always. He wanted to know if you were afraid to come to school. Afraid of him. Hah. Know what I told him? I told him to soak his head in a tub of snot. I told him it'd be an improvement."

"Yeah," Alex said. He could just picture Candy, his eyes bright, his face shiny, mouthing the sort of

131

insult that would be natural for someone with a whole, healthy body. "Gwen asked about you. She likes you."

"Nah, she's just being nice," Alex said.

"No, really," Candy insisted. "Go for it, Sport. You only go round once. Live! Live!" Then he jumped to another idea. "Hey, did you see Eddie's mother on TV last evening? My God. Two kids missing. It must be hard — not knowing whether your kids are alive or dead."

"What did she say?"

"Oh, you know. Like, if you have any information come forward, like that. Then on that same news program, they had a story about child smut."

"Child smut? What's that?"

"Oh, you know," Candy said.

"No, I don't. What's child smut?"

"It's like pornography. Except they use kids. You know, like pictures of kids doing it." Candy hurried through his explanation.

"Doing it?" Alex started to say. "Oh," he said as he began to understand. "Why would anyone want pictures of kids?"

"Well, you know. Like weirdos. Remember when you were little, they told you not to talk to strangers? Those strangers, they're the ones who like child smut."

"What are you saying? You mean maybe the strangers grabbed Deenie?" Alex asked.

"Sure, maybe. Maybe Eddie, too."

"Eddie's not a kid," Alex objected.

"Yeah, Eddie's old enough to like it," Candy said with a soft giggle.

"Cut that out, Candy. Eddie's dead. I told you that. They ought to have a funeral for him so everyone knows he's dead."

"You'd better watch what you're saying, Sport. If you're so sure that Eddie's dead, the police will want to know why," Candy warned.

"They already think I killed Eddie. I don't care. They probably think I killed Deenie, too. I think I was the last person to see her at the trailer court."

"Yeah? Did she say anything?"

"No. I think Paco, you know, the stepfather, had been belting her around — just like he did to Eddie."

"Maybe her stepfather was doing something else, too. Like, child smut begins at home."

"Yeah." Alex didn't want Candy to hang up. Dusk had settled in, but he hadn't pulled the drapes closed. Boots had left for work. Another voice sounded good. He wanted Candy to stay on the phone, to keep talking. But Alex couldn't think of anything to say. He needed to talk to someone about Eddie, but Candy didn't want to talk about death. Who could blame him? It could be just around the corner for him. Candy wasn't dumb. He knew he wouldn't live to be a grown-up. No wonder he didn't want to think about death.

"What are you doing tomorrow, Sport?" Candy asked.

"What do you mean?"

"Thanksgiving. Aren't you going to have a big deal?"

"Nope. Boots has to go to work early. How about you?"

"Oh, big deal. Lots of relatives. Mom's been cooking since Sunday. What are you going to do, then?"

"I don't know. If I feel better, I'll probably go up on the mountain. Look for Eddie some more. Scope out how it would be just to stay up there. Trap, maybe. Just cut out of school and all this police stuff. I might have to learn to live off the land. If the police charge me with killing Eddie or something, I'm cutting out."

"Living off the land isn't like going to Albertson's, is it?" Candy asked. Alex didn't realize he was being teased.

"No. It's tough to do. Even back when men could shoot game when they wanted to, none of the mountain men got fat."

"You'd probably starve to death," Candy scoffed.

Alex wanted to explain to Candy what it was like to search for piñon nuts, then take them from the cone. The resin was sticky on your fingers and smelled strong, like turpentine. Or wild grapes, or wild onions. The very air in the mountains was like food, as though it had nourishment in it. But, in the back of his mind, he knew Candy was right. He could starve to death.

"Well. It wouldn't make much difference, would it? One way or the other. Now or later, what's the difference?"

"If you don't know the difference between dead and alive, then I can't tell you." Candy sounded cold, as though he was drawing away from the phone, from the connection. Then he said, "I gotta go. My mom wants to use the phone. Hang in there, Sport."

. . .

Alex turned on the TV, then wandered into the kitchen. He stood in front of the open refrigerator, looking at the eggs, the milk, the margarine. He closed the door without taking anything out. Picking up a box of crackers from the kitchen counter, he worked his hand down through the crumpled wax paper to find only crumbs at the bottom.

He started to put the box into the garbage can and found it overflowing. Instead of bundling the garbage and taking it to the dumpster as he used to do, he walked out of the kitchen. Behind him, the cabinet door stood open, the garbage can still overflowed, and the empty box stood on the counter.

Back on the couch, he heard the name Eddie Chavez from the TV. He focused on what the newscaster was saying. "Two people have reported to the police that they were in Embudito Canyon last Friday, the day young Chavez was last seen." There was a picture of the Sandia foothills, then a reporter with two people, a man and a woman. They were both in their twenties.

Alex didn't catch their names, didn't try very hard. But he did look closely at them.

"Yes, we were panning for gold, not very far from the mouth of Embudito Canyon on Friday afternoon," the young man said. His voice issued from a bushy beard. He sounded sheepish as he explained, "We just pan for fun. Don't really find anything, you know." The woman, arms held behind her back, smiled at him and tossed her heavy-looking hair out of her face.

"Did you see anybody in that part of the canyon when you were there?" the reporter asked.

"Yes, yes. We did. There was an older couple came down. With binoculars and camera. Birders, we thought. Then it started to snow pretty heavy. It was really coming down."

He turned to the young woman. She nodded vigorously. "Then, there was a boy, or young man. Alone. With the snow, we didn't get a good look. Red-haired, we thought."

"Camouflage shirt and Levi's, we think," the woman said as though they had rehearsed their lines.

"Yes," the man agreed.

"What was he doing, this young man?" the reporter asked.

"That's what made us remember, because he was acting peculiar. He didn't come down the trail. He came down the arroyo. And he was zigzagging from one side to the other. He'd dart to a bunch of boulders, then run into a clump of willows, then out again like he was hunting for someone. He worked his way down the canyon and past where we were."

"And you didn't see him close up?"

"No, he circled around us. We were in the open by the stream."

"Did he look like he was trying to conceal himself?"

"Oh, no. Just like he was searching for something."

"Do you think he saw you?" the reporter asked.

"Oh, yes. Bound to have seen us. He was covering that ground like he was looking for a needle in a haystack. We just weren't the needle he was looking for."

"Did you, by any chance, see another boy come down alone?"

"No," they responded together.

Back in the studio, the newscaster said something about police comment. All Alex got out of it was that the police said their inquiry into the disappearance of Eddie Chavez was continuing.

Alex thought about what the couple had said. He didn't remember seeing them, or not seeing them. He tried to reconstruct that trip down the canyon. Expecting Eddie to be concealed behind every boulder or clump of trees, Alex must have looked as they described him. But — needle in a haystack? He wasn't being *that* careful. Not knowing then that he would never see Eddie again, he wasn't hunting that close. He thought Eddie might jump out at any moment.

Still, what the gold panners said was the same thing he had told the police. Eddie hadn't come off the mountain. Eddie was still up there. Dead. He was absolutely sure now.

A darkness blanketed his mind. It was too much of an effort to think about what other people saw or what the police might think. Without effort, though, his last look at Eddie replayed on his inner screen. That shaggy black hair, the whispery voice, then the golden explosion. Eddie stayed there for a second, his face already indistinct, suspended in the cloud of yellow leaves, then faded.

"I have to do something for Eddie, before I forget how he was," Alex thought. "His face is fading already." He couldn't do a funeral, he knew. But he had to do something. Something like the white cross a Mexican family puts alongside the highway when someone from the family dies in an accident there.

The cloud that was moving in on Alex's mind thickened. The effort of thinking, of planning, seemed too difficult. Saying "It doesn't matter" was much easier.

He sank back into the couch and let the heaviness drift from his head into his body. His head fell against the cushion, and his hands were so heavy he didn't think he could lift them again.

The jangle of the phone finally penetrated and he reluctantly rose to answer it. "Alex?" At first he thought it might be Boots calling from work. Then he realized it was Gwen. "Alex?" she asked again. "You sound funny."

"I'm . . . I've been asleep, I guess," Alex said.

"Are you all right? I thought you might be in school today."

"I didn't feel good enough to come."

"You didn't miss much. The day before a holiday is usually boring."

"Yeah," Alex agreed.

"Alex, what are you doing tomorrow? For Thanksgiving? The reason I'm asking, my mom and I thought, if there's just you and your mother, you might like to have dinner with us. Like, you know — you and your mom, me and my mom."

Alex didn't know what to say, didn't even com-

138

prehend what Gwen was asking. Dinner. He kept forgetting that tomorrow was Thanksgiving and families had traditions that they followed every year. Just like he had with his grandparents.

He had to say "No." Knew he couldn't say "Yes." He couldn't think of a reason. So he just said, "No, we can't."

Something stirred in the heaviness of his mind. He recalled that Gwen might know something about rituals. "Uh," Alex began, not even sure what he wanted to ask. "Gwen, what I'd like to know is . . . Well, I know Eddie's not coming back. Someone ought to have a funeral or service or something. But everyone else still thinks . . . Well, I'm the only one to do it. But I don't know any words or anything."

"You mean you really know that Eddie's gone?"

"Yeah. On TV news just now, these two people said they saw me come down, but they said Eddie didn't come down."

"What do you mean? Where were these people?"

"Right at the mouth of Embudito. Saturday when I went up, I saw where they had been panning for gold."

"If they were at the mouth, they would have to see anyone who came down the canyon, wouldn't they?" She hesitated, then said, "Could Eddie have gone around the mountain and come down Embudito Trail or Three Gun Canyon?"

"Naw. He didn't know there was any other way down. He never looked at the map. I tell you, he's still up there. He's not coming down."

"I'm so sorry, Alex. So, you'd like to do something like a ship captain does when someone dies at sea?"

Alex noticed the way she could say "dies" so easily . . . just like any other word. "Yeah, or like on TV, if someone in a Western gets it. They take their hats off and say words."

"What they usually say is something about commending his soul to the care of the Lord and may he rest in peace."

"That doesn't sound right for Eddie. He was already pretty peaceful. And happy. He was pretty happy with the way things were."

"It sounds like you might know some good words yourself, Alex. When do you plan on having your service?"

"Tomorrow afternoon, I guess. My mom has to go to work early, so I think I'll go up Embudito where Eddie and I used to hang out. I'll do it there."

· · · Chapter Fourteen

ALEX AWOKE ON the couch facing the TV. Slowly, he became aware of people on the screen bundled against the cold, their breath making little puffs of fog. " . . . Thanksgiving Day Parade . . . balloons . . . bands." Ever since he could remember, Alex had watched the Thanksgiving Parade on TV. Long ago, he had tuned out the sounds. Now he could tune out the sights and still know what was going on.

He loosened the quilt that was wrapped around him and wondered if he had spent the night on the couch with the TV turned on. He couldn't remember going to bed, or waking up when Boots came home.

He shook off some of his exhaustion and looked out the window. Her green Maverick was there, faded and looking defeated. Boots wanted a new car, wanted to live someplace else. Her life had changed for the worse when he came to live with her. When he was just a kid and he came to Albuquerque to visit, there were boyfriends and parties and knowing the right people to get a job as a dancer.

Now there was no mention of boyfriends or parties. Her life was a dull circuit of work, exercise, dancing classes, and this trailer. Alex knew she still thought of herself as young because she dressed in the kind of clothes some of the girls wore in high school. He had messed up her life, coming to live in Albuquerque.

"Hey, babe, let's go out for breakfast. It will take the place of Thanksgiving dinner. I have to be at work by dinnertime," Boots called out. She had already finished her shower and was toweling her kinky hair.

Alex turned away from the window. "Whatever you want," he said. "It doesn't matter."

"Grumpy this morning?" Boots teasingly lifted an eyebrow at him. "I should have waked you up last night and sent you to bed instead of letting you sleep on the couch."

"Did you mean to leave the TV on, too?" Alex asked listlessly.

"I don't know. Was it on? I just didn't notice." Boots was on her way down the hall to the bathroom.

From there Alex heard her yell, "Denny's or the Pancake House? Which do you want to go to?"

• • •

At breakfast, Alex cut up the sausage and pancakes. But when he put a little bit of food into his mouth it swelled into a dry, unswallowable mass. Boots seemed determined not to notice the uneaten cold food on Alex's plate, or even the dirty camouflage shirt but-

142

toned tightly across his chest. She had insisted he wash his face and comb his hair.

In her high, fast-moving voice, she told him stories about her childhood holidays, trying, Alex knew, to get him to lighten up, to soften the mask that had set on his face.

"Remember when you came to visit me at Christmas — two years ago, I think. Kenny and I were living together. You remember the big apartment with the fireplace? And you loved the cable TV, remember?"

"Yeah." Alex reluctantly was drawn into the memory. "Kenny had that red Firebird, didn't he? And he let me drive it when we were out on the ranch roads."

"Kenny was a good guy like that." Boots sparkled now that she had gotten a response from Alex.

"Did you think about marrying him, Boots?"

Boots looked surprised that Alex had thoughts like that about her. "Yes. We talked about it."

"But he didn't want to marry you because of me, huh? Is that why he didn't marry you?"

"No. Don't be silly. I didn't marry him because he didn't have any sense about money. That car was repossessed because he couldn't make the payments. He couldn't afford the rent on the apartment. Kenny was in debt over his ears on credit cards. Then he lost his job. He didn't say, but I think that had something to do with money missing from the office."

"You don't have any boyfriends since I came to live with you," Alex said. He spoke flatly.

"That's the way life is. Feast or famine. Either the phone is ringing off the hook or nobody calls. Your

143

timing was good. If you hadn't come to live with me, I'd be mighty lonely by now."

"Aw, com'on. I've ruined your life. If I wasn't here, you could afford to rent an apartment and get a better car."

"Don't be silly. I want you to live with me. I wish you could have lived with me a long time ago, but it was better for you to stay with Mom and Pop. Don't tell me you didn't have a happy childhood."

"Yeah. Sure. Except I wanted to be with you. Now that I am, I feel like I'm just a drag, ruining your life," Alex said.

"I don't want to hear that anymore," Boots said. "When I get a dancing job, I'll be making more money, and we'll move out of that dump. Everything will be better, you'll see." The pink make-up under her eyes and on her eyelids made her blue eyes positively sizzle.

• • •

On the way home they were silent. The Maverick, pulling an oily plume of smoke behind it, made so much noise conversation was always difficult. Even above the rattling of the car, Alex's gasp was audible when he saw the sign.

Juan Tabo Boulevard stretched its broad ribbons of concrete out to the south. Several pedestrian walkways arched over the wide expanse of traffic. High, handsome structures of thick timbers curved into an eye-pleasing bow. These overpasses had ramps leading to them from the cycling paths on each side of Juan Tabo. On the side of the ramp they were approaching,

144

Alex saw the sign, crudely sprayed with orange Day-Glo paint. It said: I KNOW WHO KILLED EDDIE CHAVEZ.

Even before his mind had figured out the implications of the message, his body reacted. He felt as though a karate blow from a vicious forearm had chopped against his throat, slamming him into the seat.

"What is it, Alex? What's the matter?" Boots yelled.

Mutely, Alex pointed at the sign. The next instant, they were under the walkway. Boots turned down a cross-street and parked at a strip shopping center.

"What was it? Was it that graffiti?" Boots asked.

He nodded.

"What did it say? I didn't have time to read it."

Alex took several deep breaths before he could get his throat to work. "It said, 'I know who killed Eddie Chavez,' " he finally answered.

Boots's face turned so white that the pink make-up seemed to float somewhere above its surface. "What does that mean 'I know who killed Eddie Chavez'?" She turned to face Alex squarely. Her eyes were blazing. "Is there something going on that you haven't told me?" She held Alex's wrist and by sheer will power forced him to look at her.

"No, Boots. Honest to God. You were right there at the table when I told the police the whole story. You were there when I told the others, the searchers. Every word I've said is true."

They were both quiet. She released his wrist. "I don't get it," Alex said. "Nobody believed me. They thought Eddie ran away. They thought I helped him run away. Then the people panning for gold said on the news that I came down the mountain by myself. They said I was looking behind rocks and stuff. They told the story just the way I did. Exactly like I said."

Alex stopped talking. He was exhausted with thinking things through and putting them in words. Something forced his mind to go on. "That part — the part the gold panners told about — showed I was telling the truth. You'd think the police would know I'm telling the truth about everything that happened Friday. But they do this. Put that sign up there."

Boots stared at him with her brows pulled down over those deep-set eyes. "Wait a minute, babe," she said. "The police wouldn't do that. That's not the way they operate."

"Not the police?" Alex said. "Someone else? Someone who believes Eddie is dead."

"Someone who believes you," Boots said, her voice dry and edgy. "You've been going around telling people — you told me — that Eddie was dead. Who else did you tell? Who would do a thing like that? Write something like that?"

"I don't know. Someone who wants to scare me, I guess. They — someone — mean they think *I* killed Eddie. There's no one else they could mean." Alex's throat clogged up, and he was close to crying.

"Well, they're crazy. Just a sick mind. I know you wouldn't hurt a fly. I know you'd never do anything to hurt anyone."

Back at the trailer, Boots was still indignant. Finding

146

the card Officer Marlow had left, she called the police department but hung up when she found out he was off duty. "It's that outfit next door," she said, flicking her hand in the direction of the Chavez/Rodriguez trailer. "One of them painted that on the overpass."

"Aw. Boots. Who? Mrs. Rodriguez? She thinks Eddie's alive. She wants him back home. The boys, too, I think. And Deenie wouldn't do it. She's got problems of her own," Alex said.

Boots pounced on that. "What do you mean? Problems? What kind of problems?"

Alex hadn't meant to let that slip out but now that it had, he might as well tell her. "I think Paco Rodriguez has been beating up on Deenie."

"That little girl? How do you know?"

"The last time I saw her she had a busted lip. Also, Eddie said Paco hit him." There — he'd told Eddie's secret. It didn't matter anyway. With Eddie dead, nothing much mattered.

"I didn't hear you tell the police about that."

"When I was talking to them, I thought Eddie might be alive, and I didn't want to trash Eddie's family."

"You know it gives the kids more reason to run away from home."

"Yeah. I thought of that. But I knew Eddie didn't run away from home. Right now, I know he's on that mountain, dead," Alex said.

"Quit saying that, Alex. That's why someone wrote that sign, because you've been going around saying Eddie's dead."

The ringing phone interrupted them. Boots an-

147

swered and Alex heard her anxious voice say, "Pop, how are you? How's Mom?"

She talked with him and then with her mother and didn't say a word about her son. Then she said, "Here, you talk to him," and handed the phone to Alex.

"Good news, Alex. Your grandmother's OK now. She's right here cooking Thanksgiving dinner. Well, of course, now, the dinner was sent over from the kitchen here at the retirement center. But, anyway, she's as sassy as ever. I'll let you talk with her in a minute. Right now, I want to know something about you. I was reading the Albuquerque paper. You know, just to keep up. I read about Eddie Chavez disappearing. Would that be the same Eddie you wrote about in your letter? The one you said was your friend?" Pop's voice was as raspy and strong as ever. Alex wanted to turn all his problems over to his grandfather. Just put them in his hands and wait, as he had when he was a little kid, knowing Pop would think of something.

Alex told the whole story to Pop. When he finished, Pop said, "I think you've got it figured out, son. You know how to track and if you say Eddie didn't walk off that mountain, then I reckon he didn't. Seems to me you can't do much more than what you've done."

Alex felt empty. Somehow he'd expected something like magic. Maybe Pop was too far away. Maybe he didn't understand how serious this was.

"But Pop, that sign. Someone thinks I killed Eddie Chavez."

"Some damn fool who's too smart for his britches

put that there. It could just be some joker who saw the story on TV, and doesn't even know your name or anything about you."

"What am I going to do, Pop?"

"Just like you been doing, son. Just keep telling the truth. You've got the right stuff. You can handle this." A jovial tone came into his voice, "Say, your grandma wants to talk with you."

Alex heard his grandmother's voice. "Alex, we miss you so. I hope your mother will let you come visit during your Christmas holiday. You'll like it here. Yes, we can have young people to visit, but not to live with us. But you know, you're just like our son. I suppose you've grown a lot. Oh, I can hardly wait to set eyes on you again."

Alex turned the phone over to Boots and settled onto the couch again. He thought, "Nothing's really changed. Just telling Pop about it hasn't changed anything. Eddie is still dead. And somebody thinks I killed him."

• • • Chapter Fifteen

BOOTS WATCHED ALEX pack. He stuffed his parka, canned food, matches, and flasks of water inside and strapped his sleeping gear to the outside of the pack. She shrilled at him, "What do you think you're doing? You're still sick. You can't go up there. Whatever happened to Eddie will happen to you. It's dangerous. You can't go alone."

"I've got to go, Boots," Alex said quietly. "There's something I've got to do."

"Even if I tell you not to, you're going to go? And you're going to spend the night up there, aren't you?" Boots sprayed her words like machine-gun fire.

"I've got to do it, Boots. Don't try to stop me, please." Alex couldn't explain to himself how he felt. He didn't understand it. Didn't understand what it was he had to do for Eddie. But he did pat the hard metal object in the bottom pocket of his pack. Paco

Rodriguez's gun, the small 22-caliber automatic. It was a necessary part of his equipment.

. . .

Alex's legs were still weak from the long pumping bike ride up through the city streets to the trailhead for Embudito Canyon. Strength had drained out of him while he was lying around with a cold. Also, his backpack was much heavier than any he had ever carried on a bike before.

After he hid his bike in the arroyo downstream from the big city water tank, Alex adjusted the pack on his back and tightened the belt around his hips. He started up the trail.

Soon the trail climbed up the bank and away from the stream. Alex left it and wound through the clumps of willows in the bed of the arroyo. When he stepped on the crackled ice on the stream, the sound was of delicate screaming.

As Alex climbed, his thoughts were as weighty as the backpack. Eddie was dead, and it was Alex's fault. Not the way the police thought, but dead because Alex hadn't been smart enough or grown-up enough to help him.

Alex was a drag on Boots, no matter what she said. His grandparents didn't have room in their lives for him.

He'd made a mess of school and couldn't go back. If Gwen found out what he was really like, she wouldn't be interested in him.

He was worthless. No good to anyone. Bad news for anyone in his life. Even Candy. Candy could be dead right now from that stupid fight. Alex would be guilty of the death of two friends then.

It would be better if Alex didn't come back from the mountain, if he just died before he did more damage.

A few weeks earlier, the leaves had showered on Alex and Eddie like golden coins, a shower of false promise. Now, the snow speeded the rot of the moldered leaves. Soon they would feed the black skin of the mountain. Their woody acid odor repelled and tantalized at the same time.

Alex stopped several times to rest and listen. If there were other people in Embudito, they were unusually quiet. Most people were probably at home eating turkey.

Up he went, climbing over boulders, stepping around the ice-entwined waterfalls that spouted down the sharp decline. The arroyo leveled out, and Alex was striding out on the old trail when he caught a whiff of death — of putrid flesh.

Reluctantly, because he feared what he might find, he retraced his steps. Slowly, he moved back and forth until he had located the exact cloud of molecules that held the scent. When he moved to the right the odor got stronger, more repulsive. His eyes searched before each step.

He almost stepped into a mass of leaves when he realized here was a nonleaf shape. His eyes picked out the carcass of a coyote, lying on its side, its legs stretched out in front and back as though it had died right in midlope. Its buff-colored coat melded into the leaves. All the sheen of life was gone.

Was it the same one Alex had seen on Saturday? The one that sized him up so boldly and then drifted into the buffalo grass? What had killed it? Alex couldn't tell if it was so old as to have died of old age. He didn't see any wound marks. Maybe poison. Maybe a bullet hole on the underside.

Again, Alex felt the terrible nameless weight pressing on him. He wanted to sit down and give in to it, let it push through him until he was heavy and mindless. Let it take over his body and squeeze out all his feelings and thoughts. But he fought to hold control of his mind and went on.

At The Flats, Alex pushed his pack inside the lean-to. He walked down the slope to the side of the stream and the big fir. Slipping under the drooping branches he looked intently at the sign:

SANDIA MTN. TRAPPERS
& GOLDMINING CO.

The boards were dry even though the fir dripped with heavy moisture. Everything here had lost its life. The aspen trees were bare. Ponderosa needles fell in dried clumps covering last year's cones. Even the sign had lost its magic. It looked faded and dumb — a kid-thing.

Alex selected a fist-sized rock and with it knocked the sign off the tree. Prying apart the two boards, he rearranged them into a cross and tied it with a bit of nylon cord from his pocket. On the unused side of the crosspiece, he gouged out the letters *EC*.

Leaning the cross against the base of the big Douglas fir, he looked at it uncertainly. He left it there and tried to think of something to say or do. It wasn't right what Gwen said they did in the old movies. Who was he to commend Eddie's soul to God? God could take what He wanted. Could take Eddie's soul, and the coyote's, and even Alex's whenever He wanted.

The tops of the ponderosas shushed in the wind. Above that sound, the piñon jays screeched coarse warnings. Someone was coming up the arroyo. Alex climbed out of the arroyo and stood watching the edge of The Flats. He stood very still, so that the rustle of his clothes wouldn't override other sounds. A whistle, sharp, like a signal to a dog, cut through the air.

Alex saw the dog first, its creamy chest like a shield. The German shepherd came from the cluster of aspens. Its ears stiffened as it looked around. It was following a scent. Behind it someone stepped from the trees and came surely up the leaf-covered path. The dog trotted in front of a slim figure which was wearing a khaki jacket and pants. The rolled-up legs showed hiking boots with scarlet laces. There was a brown felt hat, a hat that might have been a man's. But no man would wear it that way. Under the droopy brim, Alex saw a sweep of reddish-brown hair. Finally, his brain made the connection, and he knew it was Gwen.

She moved slowly, her eyes searching the trail ahead

154

of her. Alex wasn't sure at what instant she saw him, but he sensed she did. By a snap of her fingers, she kept the dog by her side even as it caught sight of Alex and tensed.

At last Alex stepped away from the embrace of the lean-to. "Hi," he yelled. "Over here." There was no need of that. Gwen headed straight for him.

When she got closer, Alex could see the quirky smile that pushed into her cheek. Her gray eyes leveled at him like a rifle barrel. "Mind some company?" she asked. To the dog, she said, "Justin," and pointed down. The dog sat on the approximate spot where she pointed. It was alert, eager, as though it wanted to get close to Alex and sniff him over — match him up with the scent it had been following up the mountainside.

"No," Alex said. He thought it sounded too curt, too grudging, so he added, "Come here. I want to show you something." He led her down the embankment and showed her the cross at the base of the tree. Justin, released from its spot by the snap of a finger, trotted alongside Gwen.

The girl looked at the cross, traced the letters with her finger, then straightened and looked at Alex with a wide-open intensity that made him nervous and itchy. "Yes," she said, "that's good. Have you done anything else?"

"No," he murmured. He explained how he didn't think the commending-souls words were the right thing for Eddie.

"You don't have any idea where Eddie might be?"

Alex stiffened and didn't answer her. She didn't believe him either. Maybe the police had sent her up here.

"I thought you and your mom were going to have a big Thanksgiving dinner. How'd you get to the trail head?" he asked.

"Mom drove me. She'll pick me up later. We're going to have dinner at about six o'clock." Gwen knew what he was driving at, but she didn't act defensive; nor did she seem to be trying to quiet his suspicions.

"I've been thinking. Alex, remember you asked if I could predict where Eddie could be found? I can't, you know. No one can. That was just a kid-thing, wanting to be a diviner."

"It's sort of powerful, you know. If you knew what was going to happen, maybe you could control it. But if you change it, then your prediction was wrong."

"But you knew I was going to be here in Embudito today," Alex said.

"Yes, because you told me." Gwen laughed.

"You said you want to be a poet, too. Isn't it good to know how people feel if you're going to write poetry?"

"Sure," Gwen said, "and I'm not going to give that idea up."

"My dad wrote poetry," she said abruptly.

"Dad?"

"Yes. He's dead now. He had leukemia and then killed himself. At first I couldn't forgive him for leaving me. But I understand now."

"What do you mean?" Alex asked.

"Well, I guess, when I was younger, I thought he had control, but he didn't. The disease took him. He just made a decision to cut off the suffering at the end. He thought he was saving Mom and me some pain."

"You feel OK about it now?"

"Well, I'd rather have him alive. But I understand that it's part of the pattern of living. Like winter and spring, like growth and decay."

She shrugged and looked apologetic, as though she hadn't meant to get so heavy.

Reaching into the pocket of her parka, she brought out a folded scrap of paper.

"I thought this might do for Eddie. What do you think?"

Alex took the paper, but he didn't really look at it, just saw that it was a poem. Gwen knew more about poetry than he did. "Yeah, a poem would be good," he said.

"Where would you like to stand? Is there a special place?"

"This'd be good, right here."

Alex handed the paper back. "You read," he said.

In her clear voice, Gwen read:

" 'NOTHING GOLD CAN STAY,'
by Robert Frost
Nature's first green is gold,
Her hardest hue to hold.
Her early leaf's a flower;

But only so an hour.
Then leaf subsides to leaf.
So Eden sank to grief,
So dawn goes down to day.
Nothing gold can stay."

How could Gwen know what was in his head? How could she know that in his last look at Eddie, Eddie had seemed suspended in a golden cloud? Gwen had some magic in her. "Nothing gold can stay." It felt right to think it, felt right to say it. " 'Nothing gold can stay,' " he said. "I like that."

A quiet floated between them. "I don't get all the meaning," he said at last.

"I don't either. But I think it's like Eddie's an early leaf that's the tender yellow when it first unfolds, but it can't stay that gold color, because nothing gold lasts. He was a good person, wasn't he? Maybe too good to last?"

"You mean like they say, the good die young?"

"Something like that. What do you think?"

"I think it was a good poem to say. It sounded right. Could we put it right here on the marker?" He folded the scrap of paper and wedged it between the two pieces of wood.

"Are you feeling better now?" she asked.

"Yeah, some."

Looking at her watch, Gwen said, "I have to go back down soon. Why don't you come with me? Mom can drive you to your house, or you can come and have dinner with us."

158

"No, I can't. There's something I've got to do."
Alex dug with the toe of his Reebok at a mound of
leaves.

"Did you see the sign on Juan Tabo Boulevard?"
he asked abruptly.

"What sign? There are lots of signs."

"The graffiti spray painted on the overpass. It says,
'I know who killed Eddie Chavez.' "

She gasped. "What does that mean?" she asked.

"Someone thinks I did it," Alex said bitterly. "You
and your mom wouldn't want to ask a murderer to
dinner, would you?"

The gray eyes clouded with confusion. "Murderer? You?" She spoke lightly, but Alex thought she
moved a step away from him, nearer to Justin.
"You're invited. Just remember that." Then she
added, "Who could have written that?" There was a
long silence.

"Alex." She looked down at the earth between them
and at the dog waiting patiently. Then she brought
those level eyes to beam directly into his and started
again. "Alex, you know I work at the Children's Hospital? I'm only a volunteer. But still, I learn a lot. Like
some of the kids — they get depressed. They think
they're never going to get better. Like my dad. They
think there's no use in living. They want to . . . they
try to kill themselves." She was looking at him now
as though she could see past his eyes, into his brain,
maybe into the pit of his stomach.

Alex broke the hold of her eyes and looked down
at his feet. "Alex," she said, and she laid a hand on

159

his sleeve, trying to make him look at her. "Alex, are you thinking about hurting yourself?" she asked.

He was surprised again at her insight. He ducked his head even farther so as to shield his thoughts from her. He didn't think he meant to hurt himself. He did know why he was carrying that pistol. He just hadn't put a name to his action yet. It was no good for killing animals, only people. Alex knew that. But it wouldn't hurt. No. Afterward, the hurt would be all gone.

"Naw," he said. "I'm all right. Just shook up about Eddie, is all. And about that sign."

"Alex, come down with me," she urged. "Let's get your pack." She started toward the lean-to. Alex stepped in front of her.

"I'm all right," he said. "Why don't you just go on home with your mom and have a normal Thanksgiving. Just forget about me."

She gave in to his stubbornness and started down the trail. Justin looked back as if expecting Alex to change his mind.

After Gwen left, Alex sat in the shelter. It was just a slanted wall with a short overhang on the top. Green moss covered the old split logs, and holes gaped overhead. Alex couldn't say why he preferred the dark interior to the dry boulders nearby. He didn't even know why he kept himself so tightly buttoned into his camouflage shirt.

Around him he spread out his goods from his backpack. What did he have in mind when he packed all this? He didn't quite know. Was this the big break? The break from school and from an ordered future with more school and then a job for which the school prepared him? Was it the break from the police and Mr. Plemmy, who didn't believe him? From the ugly life in the trailer court with Eddie's family acting as though he'd done something terrible to Eddie? From Boots who would never be a dancer if she had to support him? From Mom and Pop who didn't want him anymore?

He was no good to anyone. Worthless. Even if he hadn't killed Eddie, he had let him die because he didn't talk the police into going on the mountain to search for him that first night. He remembered how he sat in the back of the police car wanting to believe the police. No. He actually did believe them when they said Eddie was in a warm place, that he had run away. The memory was like acid eating into him. There must have been some way he could have convinced them. Whoever wrote the sign was right. Alex did kill Eddie.

He took out the small gun and looked at it. It fit easily into his palm, and gleamed dull nickel from the cleaning Alex and Eddie had given it. He loaded bullets, twenty-two long rifles, into the clip. Pushing against the spring, he put in six. The brass jackets made a neat parallel design against the slot of the clip. Smoothly he inserted the clip into the automatic and felt the click that meant it was in place. Making sure the safety was on, Alex then pulled the slide back. When he released it a bullet was in the chamber. He slid the safety catch down and exposed the red dot. The gun was ready to fire.

"I won't be like Eddie," he thought. "I'll be easy to find."

He took off his shoes and lined them up carefully beside his pack. He spread out his sleeping bag on a ground cloth and placed the gun beside the head of it.

Then he slid into the old blue bag, stirring up the wood-smoke smells and the memories of camping trips with Pop. It felt odd, getting into a sleeping bag in the afternoon. Always before, it had been at night, after the fire had died down. Sometimes the stars overhead looked so big, like liquid drops that might drip down out of the sky. Other times, the clouds rolled restlessly back and forth like big dust-bunnies, covering the night sky, then revealing it. A tear slid from Alex's eye and ran down beside his nose. There'd be no more camping with Pop.

He stirred, angry with himself. What was he crying about? Because he wasn't a little kid now? Because he wouldn't have the good times with Pop anymore?

He untangled his arms from the cords around the hood and reached for the gun. As he held it in his hand, he thought, "Finally."

It bothered him a little that when Gwen found out, she'd think he lied to her. He thought about writing a note. For Gwen, and the people who thought he'd killed Eddie. For Boots even, who would feel guilty, who would try to take the blame for his actions. Maybe even get hysterical, the way she did for that cat she hit with the car. Also for his grandparents, to let them know that he had been thinking like a kid, that he understood why he couldn't live with them anymore.

The gun was as warm as Alex's flesh now. The same temperature as his fingers.

His eyes focused on a tiny ponderosa not three feet from his head. It was a grotesque little thing going this way and that, rooted in the merest of cracks where ice had forced apart two sections of granite boulder. Lichens had spread their acid lacy webs and widened the crack. The pine was no more than ten inches tall, but its thickened trunk showed it had been there for several years. It reminded him of Candy, making a production out of just living. The toughness, the vitality with which it forced its roots into that crevice, that was Candy. Forcing his way into a normal life. Fighting against his twisted body.

Candy. What would Candy do if he had a good body like Alex's instead of his fragile matchstick limbs? Would he destroy it? What would Candy think? Alex heard Candy's voice saying, "If you don't know the difference between life and death, I can't tell you. Live! Live!" The words echoed in the emptiness of his head. The gun grew warmer in his hand.

Abruptly he sat up and the sleeping bag came with him like a cocoon. He unzipped it and crawled out. Putting the safety back on, he released the clip from the automatic and drew it out. He ejected the bullet in the chamber. All the parts, all the pieces, lay in his hand, as warm as he was, smooth, seductive. He had to get it away from him. He started to throw the pieces into the underbrush, into the arroyo.

He stopped. He shouldn't do that. It might be found by some kids later.

He jammed his feet into his shoes. He ran up the trail. Higher up, above The Flats, the trail crossed a spill of scree. He'd throw the gun and bullets there. No one ever went below the trail there. It was too rough and dangerous.

• • • Chapter Sixteen

THE SCREE FIELD — loose gray rocks as big as a
fist — burst from the granite sides of the mountain
like feathers coming from the torn seam of a pillow.
The loose rock extended up the steep slope toward
the crest and spread out below until it reached a border of boulders and scrub oak. In their shadow a hem
of snow remained. Nothing grew on this barren nubby
expanse. For about fifty feet, the trail cut across the
scree in a narrow ribbon.

Alex rushed onto this path, unmindful of the treacherous footing. Still running, he heaved the gun away.
The stones underfoot acted like ball bearings, sliding
Alex's feet out from under him. Desperately, he tried
to catch his balance. He fell on his back and shot off
the path feet first. Arms flailing and hands clawing,
he tried to stop gravity's pull. He plowed down
through the long spill of gray rocks.

He came to a stop at the foot of the scree field, his
feet and legs jammed against a boulder. Lying quietly,

he heard dislodged rocks skip down into the trees. When all the clatter stopped, but before his rush of adrenaline died down, he wiggled toes and fingers and moved his neck.

Carefully, he raised himself on one elbow. His neck and spine seemed to be all right. He sat up and looked at his hands. They were shredded by white gouges and tears. Blood would ooze from every cut and abrasion as soon as his circulation returned to normal.

Looking through his hands, his eyes focused on something beyond them. He saw another hand. This one, lying palm down, reached out from the gray rocks. On the back, on the soft flesh between the thumb and forefinger, Alex saw two black dots. The two dots were all that remained of the sunglasses on the Chicano cartoon that Eddie Chavez had inked into his skin two months before.

Alex had risked his grandparents' disapproval a few times to see horror movies. He had seen enough to know the terror stimulated by fake blood and mangled bodies. That didn't prepare him at all for the feelings that rushed through him now.

Shock at the suddenness of his discovery. But relief, too. The uncertainty was over. Eddie was dead, just as Alex had thought. Sadness washed through him.

From the placement of the hand, Alex could figure out what had happened. Eddie had tripped, perhaps, and lost his footing. Instead of going down feet first as Alex had, he went down head first or head over heels. It was probable that he died in the fall.

Eddie, like the coyote, had stopped dead in his

tracks. One instant, in exuberant life, careless of the pull of healthy muscle. The next, a mass of dead cells going nowhere.

Eddie must have loosed enough scree to cover his body when it came to rest. On that Friday after his disappearance, Alex had looked down over this slope and seen nothing. The search party had obviously not found any evidence here either. Maybe Alex's fall had dislodged the rock so the hand was visible.

Alex looked at the hand. It was darker than he remembered, intact, dusted with gray stone powder. Briefly, Alex thought about moving the rocks away from the rest of the body. No, he decided. He didn't want to see Eddie like the coyote, killed in midleap. He wanted to remember Eddie exploding upward in a cloud of golden dust.

His next impulse was to run from the mountain, proclaim his discovery. Caution born from a week of trying to get people to believe him held him back.

He sat still at the bottom edge of the scree slope, his knees drawn up and pulled close to his chest. He didn't notice that the cuts on his hands bled onto his camouflage shirt. His blood smeared the rocks he shifted in an effort to sit up.

"I could cover up this hand and not say anything to anybody," he thought. "What will the police think when I tell them I found the body? They haven't believed me so far. They'll think I found it because I knew where it was all the time. For sure they'll think I killed him."

Alex played in his mind the scene where he would

tell Marlow or Lily Torres. Always, even as he imagined the scene, he found himself getting hot and flustered as he tried to get them to believe him. He could imagine their writing it down on the forms on those little lines. Even as he explained how the accident had probably happened, it would be squeezed into black and white.

And Eddie's mother. When he thought of telling her, "Eddie's dead, just like I said he was. Here's his body as proof," Alex had a momentary recall of that night, less than a week ago when her face was contorted like a mask.

But, not to tell. What would that mean? It would mean carrying a secret for the rest of his life. A secret he couldn't share with anyone. It would mean having his guard up against Gwen, who could almost see his thoughts. It would mean always leaving Eddie's mother and family in doubt, never being able to grieve and mourn and face the fact that Eddie was gone.

It would mean, finally, that Alex didn't have the "good stuff" in him that Pop thought he did. If he didn't tell anyone he had found the body, he would be creating something shameful in himself. Something only he knew, something he always had to hide.

Alex stood up and took a deep breath. Moving carefully so that he didn't disturb the rocks underfoot, he found a dead branch and planted it beside the hand. He covered the hand loosely with rocks to discourage animals and birds.

His camouflage shirt bound him, and he unbuttoned

168

it completely down the front, undid the cuffs, and rolled them back on his forearms.

. . .

He didn't remember the trip home, or finding the card with Marlow's number and calling him. Boots had gone to work. Alex waited alone until Marlow picked him up. Alex sat in the passenger seat of the heavy police car. At the trailhead, four more vehicles waited. One from the sheriff's office, an emergency vehicle, and two black cars without markings. After someone brought out a key and opened the lock on the access gate, the cars proceeded at a funereal pace to the city water tank.

From the emergency vehicle, a woman paramedic took out equipment and jackets. The two men from the unmarked cars looked out of place in the chamisa and sand until they changed their city shoes for hiking boots. Then they took off their jackets and ties and put on parkas. Both carried heavy-looking cases.

With Marlow and Alex leading, the group started off. Where the easy trail left the arroyo floor and climbed the side of the canyon, the sheriff's deputy stopped and said, "Why aren't we going this way? It's a lot easier than going up through this stream-bed."

Marlow looked at Alex. Alex said, "This way's faster. And it's going to be dark soon."

The deputy made some remark about its being more exercise than he liked to take after a turkey dinner.

Alex wondered to himself, "Is it still Thanksgiving? This has to be the longest day of my life."

They finally reached the place where the trail crossed the scree. Alex pointed down the slope to where he could just see the marker stick. The sun poured from the west, painting the formerly drab rocks a carnival red and causing the trees to cast long shadows across Eddie's resting place.

The emergency crew stepped from the trail as though to go directly down the slope. "No," the deputy yelled at them, "you'll start a rock slide." While the five of them edged their way down the side of the slope and came toward the marker stick from the downside, Alex and Marlow watched. One of the civilians took out a camera with a flash and started taking pictures before anyone walked into the area where Alex had ended up after his fall. When the deputy removed a few rocks, he yelled up at Marlow, "This is it. We've found him."

Marlow took Alex back to The Flats and they sat in front of the lean-to in the quiet and waited. Occasionally, they heard a raised voice or caught the whiteness of a flash.

Alex's stomach growled. "Have you had any dinner?" Marlow asked.

"No. I don't remember eating lunch either," Alex replied.

"I'm sorry I don't have anything. I don't know how long we'll be here. The doctor from the coroner's office has to examine things to help him find out what caused death."

"I know," mumbled Alex. "I knew you wouldn't believe me."

"It's not a matter of not believing you," Marlow said. "There were only two of you up here. Death is a very serious business. We have to build up an idea of what happened independent of what you tell us. If that story says the same thing as you do, then we can say your story is corroborated. If not, then ... " He let his voice dangle off into silence.

The sunlight faded in perceptible levels as though a stage curtain were being lowered. Layers of darkness lapped up from the base of the mountain.

"I suppose they have to look for the gun, too?" Alex asked.

"Yep. It's part of your story."

"Will they give it back to Paco ... to Eddie's step-dad?"

"I don't know. We'll have to wait and see."

"Yeah. I guess you think I might have shot Eddie, huh?"

"Alex," Marlow said in a very patient voice, "we check out everything. So far, everything that you've said has proved true. If you're telling the truth about the gun, that's easy to check out."

Alex's stomach growled again. "There's not much to eat up here, is there?" Marlow said. "You just can't reach out to a bush and pick off a hamburger and maybe some fries."

"No," Alex agreed. "When I was a kid, I thought you could just go into the woods and live off the land, like the mountain men used to do." He forgot that he'd held this belief until just a few hours ago.

"Yeah, it's not like the old days. You really like the outdoors, don't you?" Marlow asked.

"Yeah. I used to want to be a trapper, but I don't think so now. I don't think I want to kill things."

"Maybe you'd like to be a forester or wildlife expert, say."

"Maybe. But I probably can't go to college. We don't have much money." Alex was somber. Now that trapping was removed from his future, he felt kind of lost.

"You'll find a way. But you don't have to worry about it yet. You've got — what — three more years of high school?"

"Yeah."

Around the shoulder of the mountain, Alex and Marlow could see strong lights stab at the darkness, then they heard crunching footsteps. The little party came into view, the paramedics linked to each other by a long bundle. Marlow turned on his flashlight and he and Alex led the procession down the mountainside.

· · · Chapter Seventeen

THE WIND RIPPLED the sides of the trailer and slashed at the roof. Only the tires piled on the roof kept the wind from lifting it into the next county. How Boots slept in the midst of all that noise, Alex didn't know. He sat on the stoop, leaning against the door. Protected from the wind, he was warmed clear to the bones by the sun.

He leafed through the thin Friday morning paper. Yesterday, there'd been no mention of Eddie on the TV news. Today, there was a short back-page story in the paper. It said the body had been discovered by the companion who had first reported Eddie Chavez missing. The investigation was continuing, the report said.

Alex knew that each sentence he read was factually true. Yet he still felt that the statement pointed a finger at him as though he had done something wrong. It was hard to take.

This morning, on the phone, he'd said something like that to Gwen. Like, how it wasn't ever going to be settled so there wouldn't be any doubts about what happened to Eddie.

"Lots of things are like that, Alex," Gwen had said. "In books and movies, everything gets wrapped up neat and it's all explained. In real life, you must have already noticed, it's not like that." She sounded serious, but Alex imagined her smile quirking into her cheek.

"Yeah, well," he stuttered. He wanted to say he liked real-life situations better, sometimes. Like when someone as special as Gwen paid any attention to him. But he was much too shy for that. Even now, just thinking of Gwen made him feel warm, as though he were blushing.

He opened the door and stuck the newspaper inside. When he twisted his body, it hurt. His neck and shoulders were stiff. Big splotchy bruises covered his back and buttocks. Alex turned back the cuffs on his sweatshirt. His hands looked like day-old raw hamburger. This shirt was soft and fleecy. Still, he felt it where it touched his skin. His Reeboks were cut and tattered from Thursday's slide down the scree.

This morning a surprise package arrived from Mom and Pop. They called it a Thanksgiving CARE package. In addition to smoked turkey and other goodies, it contained a pair of hiking boots for Alex.

Alex dipped his fingers into a little can of Sno-Seal and rubbed the wax into the seams. His fingers lingered on the smooth leather. The scent of new leather made him eager to wear the boots.

He'd wear them back to the mountains. But it was going to be different now. He had to build his real life here in the city. He might work toward a career where he could be outdoors, like Marlow had said. But the mountains couldn't be the base of a fantasy life anymore. That was over.

The tip of his little finger was swollen into a purple bulb, making his right hand awkward. Comparing fingers with his left hand, Alex could see a distinct bend in the injured one. "Probably broken," he thought.

"What happened to your finger?" Bobby Chavez asked. Alex looked up, startled to see Eddie's thirteen-year-old brother standing directly in front of him.

"I fell up there, on the mountain," Alex said, without elaboration. He didn't know where he stood in the Chavez family's regard.

"Deenie came back," Bobby said abruptly.

"Yeah? Where's she been?" Alex was a little surprised that Bobby was talking to him. The family knew about Eddie. Marlow had talked to them Thursday evening after he had brought Alex home. Not wanting to frighten Bobby away, Alex let him lead the conversation.

"She's been to Stella's house all this time." Bobby sounded disappointed that Deenie hadn't used her time to strike out for more exciting parts.

"How did Stella keep it secret?" Alex asked. Bobby

grinned. They both knew Stella's reputation for being a motor-mouth. The younger boy scuffed at the dirt with his shoe, then sat down on the bottom step, below Alex.

"Deenie left, you know, she left because of Paco." He paused and dipped his finger into the small can and rubbed the grease with his thumb.

"Yeah, he beat up on her, didn't he?" Alex asked.

"Yeah. More than that. He made her stay home from school. Then he tried to make her act, like, you know, like they were married. When she said she was going to tell Mom, he beat her." Bobby turned his wide dark eyes toward Alex to see if Alex understood what he was getting at.

"Anyway," Bobby continued, "Stella's mom went to the social worker and told her. Stella's mom told my mom that it's not fair that my mom keeps losing kids because Paco is such a bastard. See, that's when, you know, we thought Eddie ran away, too, because Paco decked him."

"Yeah, well, he talked about it. But he didn't want to leave you guys. He wouldn't run away."

"Did you tell the police about Paco hitting Eddie? Or Deenie?"

"Naw. It's none of my business," Alex said.

"Paco said you did. He said you were bad-mouthing him. Then he said Deenie was lying. And my mom got so mad. She said, 'See that door over there? You got two minutes to get your ass out of it. You're not gonna stay around here and molest my kids.' " Bobby recited all this with great satisfaction. A pleased little grin played around his mouth.

They sat in silence for a while, Alex rubbing the excess wax off his boots and Bobby hugging his skinny legs.

"Those are good boots," Bobby said. "You can wear them up in the mountains."

"Yep."

"Maybe I can go with you, now that Eddie's not . . . um you know."

"Maybe, sometime. As soon as I'm sixteen, I'm going to get a part-time job. I won't have so much time then." Bobby looked disappointed. Alex added, "Yeah, I'll take you. If your mom'll let you go."

"She will. The police told her it looked like you were telling the truth all the time. He said — the officer said — it looked like Eddie died in an accidental fall. He said they're doing an — what do you call it? Like examining the body?"

"Autopsy?" Alex supplied.

"Yeah. That's it. Did you see him, Alex, when they dug him out?"

"Naw. Just his hand, that's all."

"Sometime, take me to see where it happened, OK?"

"Sure. I put a marker there for him. I'll show you that, too."

· · ·

For Alex, the marker wasn't too important. In his mind, he could bring back his last look at Eddie. That

black-figured leap upward into the golden explosion
of aspen leaves. Eddie hanging suspended between the
earth and the sky.

> *Nature's first green is gold,*
> *Her hardest hue to hold.*

DATE DUE
